PRINCESS SOJOURN

THE AZURE SERIES

A.L. HAWKE

PHANTOM HEART, LLC

ISBN: 978-1-953919-67-0 (ebook)

ISBN: 978-1-953919-86-1 (paperback)

ISBN: 978-1-953919-89-2 (hardcover)

Library of Congress Control Number: 2024924686

Line edited by Stephanie Marshall Ward

Proofread by Alexa B., alexabooks.wixsite.com/authors

Cover © 2024 by BRoseDesignz

Map Design © 2021 by Sean Counley

Published by Phantom Heart, LLC

27702 Crown Valley Pkwy D-4, #201

Ladera Ranch, CA 92694, USA

Printed and bound in the United States of America

First printing December, 2024

Learn more about A.L. Hawke at www.alhawke.com

Correspondence: contact@alhawke.com

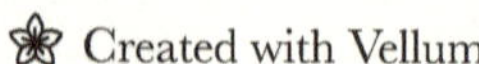 Created with Vellum

For my daughter
My princess and angel

The Ambrosia Dynasty

The Amazon nymphs of Azure Blue lived longer life spans than humans.
Legend claims Queen Danaë lived for over three centuries. This family tree spans over half a millennium.

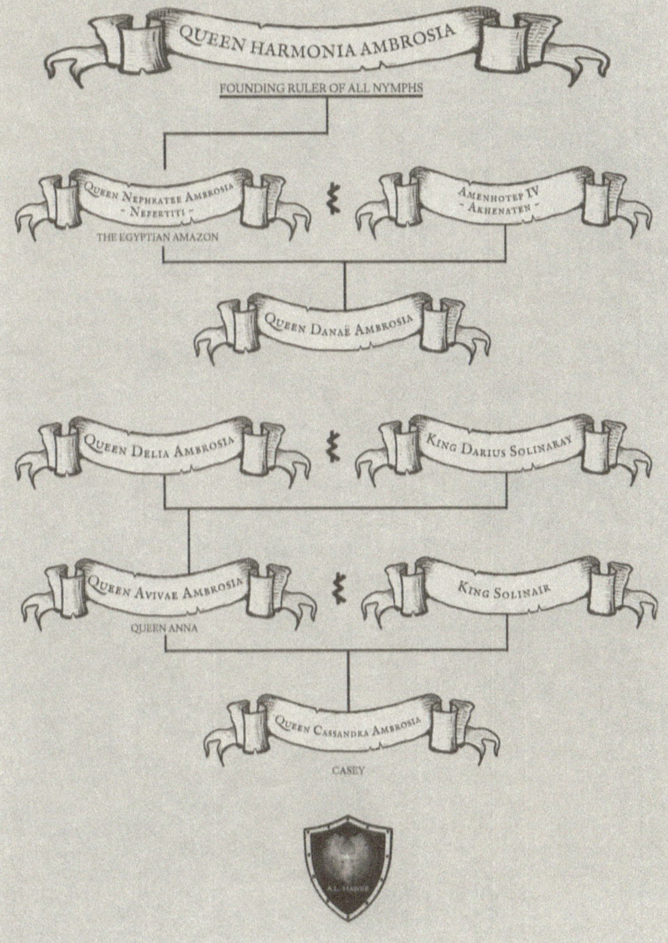

MOUNT AMBITUS
THE STRATOS RIVER
Napea
AZURE
THE CRYSTAL PALACE
Tartarus
Elysium
River Styx
THE UNDE

The Hinterland
Southerland
RE BLUE
THE STYGIAN HOLE
STRAIT OF AZURE
THE LANDS OF ATALA
Mangoria
Mount Ambitus
ylum Caves
Hypnos
er Styx
NDERWORLD

VISITORS FROM THE YELLOW LAND

FRENZY IN THE COURT TURNED INTO MADNESS WHEN IMADA spotted the first sails being hoisted near the yellow shores across the Strait. I climbed up the highest watchtower, so excited, and looked down over our ramparts, beyond our blue-green forest, to the purple coastline to catch the first ship landing on our shore. Well, no ships had arrived yet. But there sure was a lot of commotion in the purple grass below. Today our violet field wasn't purple. It was red, the color of all the tents my people had erected in preparation for the festival. I caught three Amazon nymphs rushing over our great wooden drawbridge with their arms packed with supplies. Others raked leaves, trimmed flower bushes, or walked our winged unicorns through the blue-green field near the main amphitheater.

Meanwhile Cambria surveyed everything around our castle walls, wearing her scarlet hoplite armor, atop her fierce brown winged unicorn, Ranun. She was jumpy, snapping at everyone, hurrying their final preparations. In the center of our grassy field was a huge open wooden stadium beside a number of far larger red tents. More Amazon nymphs rode on flying unicorns, kicking up blue dust as they trotted around the stadium. Other nymphs, sitting on the benches, hoisted our phoenix standard on poles. I leaned forward on the stone wall to gaze at the roof of the Northern Tower. Here was the largest flag in the kingdom. No doubt the incoming ships would see it over this crystal tower when—

"Avivae!" Engel snapped, throwing open the wooden door behind me. "Avivae, why aren't you in Court!"

I nearly fell off the wall. That little blue dwarf was so mad. He snorted through his broad nose and stomped on the ground. He was always mad about something. Then he waved his stubby finger toward my face.

"Young lady, you need to get down now! Everyone is waiting."

I laughed. Sweet, sweet Engel. Engel was a Mandrigel dwarf with purple-tinged skin—a far darker shade of blue than mine —two heads shorter than me, wearing a silky-smooth purple tunic and small black boots. He was the kindest man you could ever know. But he always seemed ruffled over something. I kind of liked it when he got upset. His cheeks would turn bright purple. Then he would snort through those large nostrils, and his bright blue eyes would bulge. His stubby little hands would grip each other, and he would jump up and down. He'd get so cute.

"Don't sneak up on me like that, Engel. I nearly fell off the wall."

"You have to get downstairs, princess, now!" he cried. "Queen Delia wants you to stand beside her to greet the king."

I looked down at my lovely white lace dress, which I had worn the previous night at our preparation supper with Mother. Mother, of course, didn't approve, but she was too busy worrying over every detail of this morning's ceremony. I straightened the wreath of flowers on my head.

"When?"

"*Now!*"

"Calm down, Engel. What's the rush anyway? I haven't spotted them reaching our shore yet."

I glanced back toward the Strait of Azure. *But then I saw them!* Green sunlight sparkled over something far off in the violet water. It was a ship! I finally could make out a ship with sails approaching the shore.

"They're here, Engel!" I cried. "Look! Look! They're here!"

Engel forgot everything and hobbled to the wall. But he was too short, so I had to lift him up. And then we both gazed out past the fields, past our forest, and beyond the amethyst beaches to the sea.

Engel looked up. It was cloudy and a haze shrouded the bright green sun. "They're crossing just in time," he said, forgetting all his anger. "Hmm, but looks like the weather might not be so favorable tonight. It would be Poseidon's pleasure to ruin your mother's festival. Oh, put me down!" he exclaimed, shaking his head. "Come on. Move it, Avva! Get downstairs now, princess!"

"Is that any way to talk to a princess?"

"Now, Avivae! Now!"

The inner Court was as festive as the outer, being loud and full of all kinds of raucous banter, with women's voices laughing and shouting. And the chatter and laughter got crazier when I approached the two heavy wooden doors of our throne room. Two guards in scarlet stood at attention. When they recognized their princess, they smiled and opened the doors for me.

Engel had been right. I was late. Very late. Three hundred of my sister Amazon nymphs were already sitting on rows of wooden benches in the Court, murmuring and giggling with one another. Far, *far* worse, they all stopped everything they were doing and turned excitedly to stare at me. They had anticipated the grand entourage of visitors, so when they saw that it was just their princess, they burst into laughter. That made me feel so stupid.

I straightened my peplos, doing my best to ignore them, as I made my way down the central aisle. At the end of the Court, Mother was sitting on her golden dais, over three marble steps, glaring at me. Like me, she was formally adorned in darker blue makeup to accentuate the natural blueness of our nymph skin. And she had on a black head-dress and a lovely sparkly violet dress.

The Hall was magnificent. The throne room always looked amazing, being the greatest hall in our whole palace. But now a hundred scarlet Amazon flags lined the rows of benches. And beautiful multicolored cloth streamers hung from the walls. The tall vaulted ceiling included a central glass dome, and black marble columns stood between the floor-to-ceiling crystal windows. Through the windows, we could look out upon our garden of dark-blue bushes and trees and bright cherry-red vines. It was as if we were outside. Great white marble statues of nymph heroes stood in front of the columns. And today the polished white marble of the grand central aisle was covered with a long red carpet. All the Amazon nymphs were either dressed in their finest dresses, like me, or wearing our red hoplite armor.

As I made my way down the aisle, my eyes fell on Mother. Unlike her subjects, the queen wasn't amused by my tardiness. No, not amused at all. Then everyone laughed more than ever as Mother motioned for me to hurry up and stand by her throne.

I stood on Mother's right. Cambria—her chief guard and general—stood at attention on the queen's left. She wore the red Amazon armor I had seen her wearing outside. I gazed at the crowds, looking as serious and proper as I could. Mother had lectured me all night about behaving with propriety.

That's when Engel hobbled through the entrance. Fortunately, the doors hadn't been closed yet. I smiled and, despite how embarrassed he probably felt, he smiled back at me. I loved that dwarf so much.

Then I saw my best friends Hanna, Eva, and Iris sitting on the other side of the aisle in the front row, doing their best not to snicker at me.

"Really, Avivae," Mother snapped quietly. She looked carefully about her. "I told you how important this day is. Why must you do these things? Why are you so late?"

"Sorry, I . . ."

"Forget it. Just be quiet."

Then she quickly turned back to her subjects with a fake smile.

And then . . .

The torches lining the rows of seats became brighter. The wait was so terrible. I stood so long that the green sun fell below the glass dome above. I even began seeing stars above, amid wisps of white clouds. But, unlike my friends, I knew it'd be a long wait. Leave it to Mother to have us overprepare, waiting around when their ships hadn't even beached on our shores yet. I started feeling envious of my three friends in the front row. Because they could sit down. They looked bored, but at least they were sitting. My legs hurt. My shoulders and back ached. And I couldn't stop letting my fingers fidget—or telling myself not to do that: one of the slew of orders from Mother's rehearsal last night.

I glanced back at her. Boy, she really hated me tonight.

But then her scowl vanished as the two grand doors opened again. All went completely still. And then my mother's face turned brighter than I had ever seen it.

Cambria grew a large grin too, pounding her staff on the marble floor.

"Queen Delia, I announce King Darius, the Sun King!"

And that was followed by a burst of applause as everyone turned once again to look behind them. The heraldry didn't disappoint. In walked a crowd of large men, most in glistening gilded armor. I had seen men before, but it had been so long ago. Of course, at every Olympiad, every four years, we Amazon held our games. At every festival men were allowed to visit our isle. And at the end of every festival, Mother ushered them away. Only a handful of women accompanied the men—I counted about six—all in beautiful, elegant foreign dresses. The metal of the men's armor clinked and clanged as they all walked down the central aisle. Many men held gilded shields reflecting the flickering torchlight. Others held glistening gemmed scabbards by their waists. But they all smiled and seemed excited, just as most of us were. Nearly every man had a long dark beard. Such was the fashion in the Hinterlands, or so Engel had once told me. Then, as they filled the Great Hall, I heard something I hadn't heard in ages—the low sound of men's baritone voices.

But I couldn't find their king.

A few of the nymphs in the aisles recognized some of the men and waved at them like crazy. Many had been talking for many moons about the "special man" they had met at the last Olympiad.

It was at this time when, all of a sudden, an older nymph named Kainya disregarded all formalities and burst into the central aisle and threw her arms around one of the men, kissing him like crazy all over his face and neck. We all laughed. Then the poor young girl ran back to her seat, dropped her head in her hands, and tried to hide her face in shame.

But I still didn't see their king.

Men approached the throne and fell to their knees before me. Others had to bend on a knee in the center aisle, as there wasn't room for all the visitors near the throne.

Then only one man remained standing. He didn't look much different from the others. He too wore gold metallic armor, and he had long jet-black hair, dark eyes, a small nose and mouth, and a large full beard. He approached Mother's dais and reached his hand out to her with a bow.

"Oh, Delia, it's been so long," he said, shaking his head. "Aye? Far too long." Then he walked up a step and kissed the back of her hand. "Far, far too long. But you are more radiant than ever, Amazon queen. And now there is no joy greater in my life than this moment. Our reunion."

Mother lost all her pomp, stood up, and led him up the dais steps into her tight embrace. He drew her up so close and kissed her. And then the two gazed into each other's eyes, just holding each other in silence. The Hall became so quiet again. Then the king turned to me and smirked. And then he shocked me—no, shocked all of us—by roughly gathering my mother in his arms, bending her down, and kissing her lips hard like a total beast. A few of the nymphs in the Court gasped. But Mother couldn't stop laughing in his arms. She stood on her toes and kissed him too.

The whole Court exploded in applause.

"Well, well," my mother said, backing up a little. But she didn't let go of his hand. "Well, great king, I haven't yet permitted you to step foot in my lands. Certainly not up to my throne."

She let go of him and straightened her dress. Then she seemed to be lost in a trance, staring deeply into his eyes again.

"Aye . . . "

"Aye," he said with a chuckle, gazing into her eyes. He stepped down the marble dais steps and bowed to her with a broad stroke of his arm. "Pardon me, great queen of Azure. May my men step foot on the lovely shores of Azure Blue?"

"You may, King Darius," she said with a nod. "You may." She sat back down and spoke loudly enough so that all could hear her. "We welcome all of you. Every Amazon nymph greets every man this morning. I have prepared sleeping quarters for you in tents on the fields outside the palace. We have provided the finest foods, some from the farthest reaches of Hellena, to fit your tastes. And we have myrle berry wine. We shall dance. We shall sing. And I look forward to engaging with every one of you."

"*Hear! Hear!*" cried some men. Many stomped their feet. "*Hail Queen Delia! Hail!*"

"I've seen your preparations, Azure Queen," King Darius replied formally. "It is an arduous journey from Castle Cove to your Isle of Napea. But you cannot know how happy I was that you agreed to finally hold the games in winter. My men cannot wait to compete."

"You may compete against Amazons this Olympiad, King Darius," Mother said with a nod and a grin. "But, I'm afraid, you will lose."

Many laughed.

"We shall see," he said, laughing and slapping the metal on his leg. "Aye, we will see." Then he touched the shoulder of a larger companion with a dark complexion. "Please, Delia, if I may introduce my general once more, General Onos."

Onos was the same height as the king, but with broader shoulders. The king was huge enough, but Onos was a giant, burly man. Onos had no beard and no hair at the top of his head. His skin was dark. And there was a long scar running from his cheek up to his left eye. He looked mean, but when he looked at me, he smiled.

"Welcome, general," Mother said. "Welcome. And you remember *my* general, General Cambria?"

"Aye, my lady," Onos said, bowing to Cambria. "She and I enjoyed sharing stories of battle when we arrived at the last games. I particularly enjoyed talking of your enchanted unicorns. All my men cannot wait to see the winged unicorns of Azurea once more."

"And you shall, sir," said my mother with a smile. "You shall. You and your men shall meet them firsthand in tournament with my subjects."

"I've brought my son, Marcus, to compete in the games," General Onos said with a nod. He pointed over to one of the younger men in the central aisle. A young man wearing a formal brown tunic and pants bowed. He was a tall, hand-some boy, I'd guess about two years older than me, maybe fifteen or sixteen, with short black hair, penetrating green eyes, and stubby eyebrows. He appeared small next to the men, but he was already a little taller than my mother. We nymphs are tall, but these men were not only tall in stature but much larger in girth. Marcus's skin was dark like his father's, and his face was beardless.

The boy walked closer and bowed. Then he totally humili-ated me by bowing only to me. I quickly looked away, feeling my cheeks heat up. Hanna and Iris, in the front aisle, stupidly snickered.

"You're welcome to compete, Marcus," my mother said with a smile. "I look forward to witnessing your skills."

"My queen—" The boy bowed again. "It is my greatest honor." But then he made sure to bow only to me again.

"And may I introduce you both to my daughter, Princess Avivae," Mother said.

I bowed before the king.

"Welcome to Azure Blue, King Darius," I said in the exact way I had rehearsed a thousand times last night.

"Aye," said Darius warmly. "You are looking as lovely as your mother, Avivae. My, how you have grown, princess."

And he took my hand up to his lips and kissed the back of it. For a moment, I feared he'd grab me the way he had grabbed my mother, but then he just patted my hand. His general reached for my hand and kissed it too. And then the general's boy looked at me. Again. Thank the gods, the boy didn't ask for my hand. I think I would have died if he had done that.

Mother walked back up the stairs and sat back down. Then she stretched out her arms toward the crowd, clapping loudly. That was followed by Cambria's staff thundering once more on the ground.

"The moment we have all waited for for so many moons has now arrived," Queen Delia shouted merrily. "Let us drink and let us enjoy each other's company." The Hall burst out in applause. "It shall be half a fortnight, only half, per my edict, and no longer. According to custom—brought down from our great Queen Harmonia, down to Queen Nephratee, and then to my mother, Queen Dainya, and finally to my reign—we give libations and honor to only one god for the games. Persephone. May Cora bless us all and fill each and every day of this competition with joy as we not only compete, but join with one another, our greatest friends, the men from across the Strait of Azure. The greatest men of Atala. The men of the Sun Kingdom."

And she surveyed all the rows in the Great Hall. Then she rose and gestured with both arms to the crowd.

"Let the games begin."

And then the Hall exploded, louder than ever. So loudly that I think it shook the glass dome above. All formalities were forgotten. Many couples who had spent years apart rushed into each other's arms. There was such great merriment as everyone who had done all they could to resist were finally allowed to see their loved ones after so many years.

I escaped to my friends. And after so many nymphs had jumped up to embrace their lovers, I just sat down beside my best friend, Hanna, in the now empty row to rest my legs.

2

____

DAPHNE

I had met Cambria in the stables the next day, at midday, trying one last time to convince the general to let me compete in the games. I had gone up the stable towers, the tallest points in our palace, with the excuse of needing to groom my shiny gray winged unicorn, Daphne. My unicorn hardly needed grooming. I'm with Daphne almost every day caring for her—I love my pet so much. But I knew Cambria had been tending our unicorns to ready them for competition.

Cambria said no.

That put me in such an awful mood. I felt so horrible that I decided to stay with Daphne in the evening and skip the dance.

Right now, I was on a balcony in Daphne's stable watching the turquoise sun dipping down over the horizon below Mount Ambitus. Ambitus was such a giant mountain that we could never see its peak. It looked more like a wall, always blocking off one side of our island. On the other side, in the east, clouds were forming. Engel had been wrong. A storm was brewing, and it might still spoil the games this year.

"Avva, what are you doing here?" asked Hanna. She

looked annoyed. "I've been looking all over the palace. Who disappears when men arrive?"

"You saw what happened this morning." I shrugged with a sigh. "I was humiliated by that stupid young boy at breakfast. Perhaps I don't want any more of them."

"Marcus is so cute, Blue. That was cute."

Then Hanna snatched a brush on a shelf, went to Daphne, and ran it along the unicorn's neck. "Ahh, how are you, Daphne? How are you, girl?"

The unicorn neighed.

Hanna turned with a wide smile. "Daphne's fur looks good. You've been at it all day again, haven't you?"

"Of course." And I snatched my brush back from her.

"Why are you acting blue, Blue?" Hanna asked.

Then I irritably ran my brush along Daphne's fur, a bit faster than before.

That's when Hanna's eyes turned dreamy, looking up at the tall wooden ceiling above. You know, Hanna's eyes are a much darker blue than mine, nearly violet. Well, those sapphire gems seemed to look lost all of a sudden, just like Mother's eyes when staring at the king. I knew she was thinking about men.

"Eva and I passed Marcus at the bridge a moment ago," Hanna said with a wide smile. "He came up to me because he saw you and me together. I told him you weren't paying any attention to his note and you weren't going to meet with him. You had hinted as much."

"Why would I? And the mere fact that he expected me there just because he wrote the words tells you how pompous he is."

"Yeah, well, I also told him I didn't know where you were. Of course I did. Where do you ever go? He made Debra and me laugh so much when he said, all cocky, that not seeing you by the bridge was merely a delay. He said he'd spend some time with the princess sooner or later, even though you stood him up tonight. I wonder what special gift he wants to give you?"

"I didn't stand him up. And I don't care, Hanna. I haven't even talked with him yet. He's a stranger. I never agreed to meet with him—"

"At sunset, Avva, sunset. Meeting at sunset is *sooo* romantic." She looked up at the wooden roof with stupid dreamy eyes again. "Sending that note across the table this morning in our dining hall was so romantic too."

"Passing notes down the table at breakfast isn't romantic, it's childish." I walked over to grab a heavy pail of water with both hands. "Just go walk with him along the beach yourself, if you want."

"Really? . . ."

"But . . . you wouldn't mind, would you, Avivae?"

"Why would I like an idiot?"

"He's not an idiot, Avva. He's quite handsome. I saw him practice for the games this afternoon. He was sword fighting with some of the adults. I think he's better than some of them."

"He's the general's son."

"Yeah. He's big and muscular. The general's son."

"Gallant?"

We laughed. That's what Hanna had whispered to me that morning at breakfast when he passed over the note. As if he were as gallant as my great-grandmother Nephratee, who, according to myth, fought Cerberus at the gates of Hades. Or my grandmother, who fought the Dragon of Colchis. Brave and dashing like that? Hardly.

"He's all yours."

"Really, Avva, really? You sure you don't mind? He seems stricken by you."

"Because I'm the princess. That's all. He doesn't even know me. He just likes what I am."

"I'm not so sure. He keeps looking at you."

I shrugged and grabbed a rake leaning on the wall. I moved some of the hay to one side of Daphne's stable. Then I sighed really loudly. I was so mad that night that I wasn't even in the mood for my best friend's gossip.

"I can't believe you're this angry at Marcus over his note," she said. "Just ignore him then. But Napea is full of men now, only for the games, you know. And they're all waiting to dance tonight. So why in Hades aren't you going to the dance? You plan on ignoring all of them until they return in four years? Or maybe you just fancy horses instead?"

"Stop, Hanna," I said, lightly slapping her shoulder. "Leave me alone, all right?"

"You're really gonna just stay here by your lonesome?"

"She said no. Okay?"

"Huh? Your mother said you can't go to the dance?"

"No, stupid, Cambria said no. Cambria said I can't compete in the games."

"She already told you that you can't compete. You're too young."

But that only made me more upset. I shrugged and lifted the heavy water pail with both hands. I was about to pour it in the horse's drinking well when Hanna stopped my hand.

"Come on, Avivae. Let's get out of here and have fun tonight at the dance. The Court can care for your unicorn. There are so many boys."

"Leave me alone, Hanna."

I heaved the water from the heavy pail into the well. Then I giggled as Daphne nodded her head in appreciation. I ran my hand along the multicolored horn on her head, which was glowing as it reflected the torches hanging on the walls.

Hanna pulled my arm again. "But Marcus is cute, right?"

"Hanna! Yes. Marcus is cute. So go get him and leave me alone."

But that was his cue. Somehow, at that perfect moment, Marcus strolled into the stables.

He looked silly. Hanna and I were wearing pants in the hay-filled wooden stables. Marcus had on this regal-looking white tunic for the dance, and his short black hair was slicked back. As he strode in, he looked so conceited.

"Hello, ladies."

But he did look handsome. And Hanna just about died.

"My name is Marcus." He took a knee before me. "I was disappointed that you didn't meet me at the bridge, princess." Then he reached out for my hand. I didn't give it. I just glared at him. "I expected to see you when the sun came down. I have something I want to give you. And I thought we'd walk through your wondrous fields together."

"I'm busy."

Marcus nodded. Then he gave up reaching for my hand and slowly rose.

"How'd you find me here?"

"I followed her," he said pointing. "A soldier always watches one's company in battle."

"Oh, so I'm your enemy then?"

"Such splendor," Marcus said, ignoring me. "Incredible." He petted the soft gray and white feathers on Daphne's wing. "Behold, a mythical unicorn of Azure Blue. In my dreams, when Father told me he was taking me to compete in the games this year, all I could think of were these magnificent flying beasts. How can something so beautiful be so deadly?"

"They're like Amazon nymphs."

"Magnificent," he said, still staring at Daphne.

"But my unicorn has been through a lot."

"Yes," he said, stepping back. "I noticed her back leg limps when she walks. She appears weak, yes? A bit lame."

Excuse me? A bit lame?

Hanna suppressed a laugh. But she didn't say anything. Apparently, she was too nervous to speak. Next to Marcus, she looked coy—a ridiculous thing from my not-so-shy best friend.

"I love horses," he said, running his fingers over Daphne's feathers. "But we don't have unicorns in Azerban."

Then he turned and gazed right into my eyes. He had green, almost jade, eyes and for a moment we just stared at each other, and that reminded me of the look King Darius had given Mother. Then he ran the brush along Daphne's side. But all the while, as he glanced at me, it seemed he would have preferred running his hand through my hair instead.

I blushed, thinking my blue cheeks were probably a bit red.

"Your loss, Marcus," I muttered, "your loss."

"Look, you don't mind if I call you Avivae?"

"Avva's my name," I said with another shrug. "This is my friend Hanna."

He bowed before her. Hanna nodded but still kept mum.

I grabbed my brush back and ran it along Daphne's perfect mane.

"Why not tell me of your nice horses in Azerban," I said, brushing Daphne's mane.

"Well, I wouldn't call them *nice*. Our horses are fierce fighters, Avva, bred for battle."

"What do you mean by that? You don't think Daphne is fierce? Don't think she can fight in battle?"

"No, no, I was talking about our horses. But, yeah, it's hard to believe that this creature, so beautiful and majestic, can fight."

"Why do you think she limps? Our monokera have been in many battles. The greatest of all time was Harmonia's battle in Trialga. There they swooped from the clouds as we rained arrows upon our enemies. Don't tell me about how "fierce" your horses are, sir. I guarantee you that even my injured horse can ride circles around the best of yours."

He put his hand up. "I meant no offense, princess."

"Avva," Hanna said, "I've heard that Darius uses horses very effectively in battle."

"Yes, I didn't mean it as an insult," Marcus said. "Surely your Daphne is one of the greatest horses I've ever seen."

"But she *IS* the greatest. This is the greatest steed that has ever lived, nearly matching our most treasured unicorn, Antilus. Antilus flew with our founding queen, Queen Harmonia. Daphne flew with my grandmother, Queen Danaë, battling the dragon."

"Will she be competing in the games then?"

"Why would she need to do that? It would be an insult for her to compete in the games. A legendary unicorn who once saved a hundred nymphs in Colchis hardly needs—"

"Avva," Hanna said. "He doesn't mean anything—"

But I threw my hand up to shush her.

"Queen Dainya," I interjected, feeling angry, "the third Amazon queen of Napea, battled atop this very unicorn. I tell you, any horse you have is not half as majestic as this one. If Daphne be lame, as you say, I guarantee that she's still strong enough to win any footrace against any horse of yours."

"I only commented on how she ambles, princess," he said. Then he folded his arms. "You can see she's weak in her back leg. That's all. I doubt she can run."

I turned to Hanna in amazement. "Really? You want me to show you?" Hanna shook her head. But the boy smirked.

"You doubt my words?" I asked. "My unicorn once fought with the Amazons of Colchis, I tell you. Daphne had to battle Zeus himself. She stood up to a dragon. Have you heard of dragons? What mighty horse does your king own that can fight a dragon? Daphne is the greatest steed that has ever lived."

"All right, I believe you. I meant no offense."

"You're an idiot," I said with a nod. Because he didn't look like he believed me.

"Avva!" snapped Hanna.

"This horse is lame, princess," Marcus said, shrugging.

"That's all. Whatever she did in her past, she's clearly injured—"

"Stop calling her lame! She is perfectly capable of running and competing!"

"Marcus," Hanna said, "you don't understand. Daphne means everything to Avva and—"

"One lame monokera bests any of your horses any day, Marcus," I interrupted. "I guarantee it."

But he infuriatingly grinned and nodded with his arms folded.

"Would you like me to show you?" I said, growing a sly grin. "We can take her out tonight? How 'bout that?"

"Avva," cried Hanna, shaking her head. "What are you doing?"

"I'm proving that Daphne's strong enough to run circles around him."

"But, Avva," Hanna said, "Daphne *is* weak. She's injured. Just leave this alone. You don't have to prove anything to him."

I sure do. Look at his smirk.

"Tonight?" he asked.

"Why not?"

"It's raining."

"Oh, I'm sorry, does the rain frighten you?"

"Well, I'm supposed to return to Father soon," he said with a laugh. "But . . . all right, if you think it won't be long, sounds like fun. I'd love to witness your mighty horse in action. Why don't you gallop through the field below, and I'll watch from one of the balconies on the tower here. It would be a dream for me to watch a monokera in action."

"Oh no. You and Hanna can come along with me. We can fly to the Stratos under Mount Ambitus. That should be far enough—"

"*The Stratos, Avva!*" cried Hanna. "*By air on Daphne!*"

"All three of us atop this horse?" he asked, amused.

"Sure. Hanna and I don't weigh much. And you're young and thin enough, not too much to weigh her down."

"I don't think we should, Avva," Hanna objected. "It's really starting to rain. This is crazy."

"I am crazy, Hanna," I said, still staring challengingly at Marcus. "You know I am."

"By my honor, princess," the boy said, gesturing with an extended arm toward the exit with more smugness. "By all means, lead the way."

But then, oddly, at that very moment it seemed to rain harder than ever.

3

A PRINCESS'S SOJOURN

As the wind rushed over my cheeks and hair, I turned back and laughed at the sight of the boy's bulging eyes as we hurdled over the edge of the balcony into the foggy night. Marcus was not one to look afraid, but I finally saw terror in his eyes. Hanna looked frightened too. She had flown a thousand times, but I think she was worried about Daphne. My unicorn *was* injured, and it was storming pretty hard. And I don't think anyone had taken Daphne much farther than a league in the clouds in over a century, certainly not in the middle of a storm. That was why Mother had given her to me at such a young age. She had not expected anyone to fly her.

Thunder cracked and lightning flashed. Below, the black and gray fields flared a lovely sapphire with each strike. We circled over the Crystal Palace. During the day, under the green sun, it shone azure and emerald. Under clouds and moonlight, it just glowed a lovely white. But even that glistening white light was beautiful.

After some time, I felt the grip of my two companions loosen. I looked back and Marcus had regained his usual conceited composure. Instead of showing fear, he gazed down at all the roads and buildings beyond the walls of the palace in awe.

We passed the palace walls. Many of the scarlet tents on our grassy fields were now glowing from inner fires, no doubt keeping the guests warm as they took shelter from the rain. I imagined that had it not been raining I probably would have spotted many nymphs in the purple field, walking hand in hand with the men.

"Where shall we go, princess?" shouted Marcus, behind me, laughing.

"The Stratos," I shouted. "I can show you—"

"The river is too far, Avva!" objected Hanna.

"I want to show him the ruins," I said.

"By all means," shouted Marcus heartily.

The Stratos wasn't too long a flight, but if it stormed harder, it could take half the night for Daphne to navigate through the wind and rain. I figured I'd go a little farther and decide if we had to turn around.

"Are you doing all right, girl?" I asked Daphne, patting her wet feathers. Her breathing was a bit labored, but she bucked her head back and neighed, happy to be roaming free.

Behind me, Marcus and Hanna were now looking down at the great wooden amphitheater directly below us.

"I hope the rain doesn't muddy the training grounds too much for our sword fight," Marcus said. "I plan to compete tomorrow."

"These storms usually clear fast enough, Marcus," Hanna hollered.

"Hope so," Marcus replied. "But that is why the games usually are in the spring, right? Well, I must say, I would never have expected such adventure tonight, princess! This is such great fun!"

Daphne didn't disappoint. She might have had an injured leg, but she swooped through the gale and darted over the dark-blue woods toward the great Mount. In no time, we approached the base of Mount Ambitus. Through sharp, icy rain and wind, I found a spot in our blue-green forest beside the Stratos River.

We landed on the mountainside. On the other side was our lovely glowing blue river.

But the minute we hit the ground, the rain fell harder than ever. The purple and blue woods were thick in this land, so all three of us leaped off Daphne and ran for shelter. Then, after we spent a moment catching our breath, I led my companions down a thickly wooded path that paralleled the river. We tried to stay under as much shelter as we could, but it was impossible to avoid getting wet. I held Daphne by her damp wing as Hanna and Marcus trailed behind.

Soon we slowed to a hike as we began climbing a muddy path. There was enough of a canopy of trees and branches here to keep us dry.

As we walked, I educated my human companion on the glorious past of my people. I told him that this blue-green woodland was the ancient home of the Amazon. In ancient times, the nymphs ate and slept in trees. They hunted and gathered with simple stone tools and lived along the waters in peaceful ignorance, until my great-great-great-grandmother Harmonia freed them. Harmonia studied man's civilization, even living for a time with men across the Strait, and she returned and taught my people about culture, the shield, and the sword. Then she built the first Amazon city here.

The rain calmed.

Soon Hanna was hiking beside me through blue brush up a narrow rocky ridge while Marcus enjoyed falling back and admiring Daphne. Despite all his pomp, I liked that he was so impressed by my winged pet.

"It's getting cold, Blue," Hanna said quietly by my ear. "We should be home beside a nice fire. You don't need to impress him anymore."

"He makes me so mad," I whispered back. "I don't think I like him."

"Forget him. Let's just go home."

"We're almost up the trail, Hanna. We might as well just show him the ruins. They're right over the hill."

"But Avva, what if it starts pouring again? We have to be able to get back soon."

As the trail leveled, a stream blocked our path. There was a fallen tree trunk large enough to balance on. Raindrops fell on the glistening river and its tributaries and streams, which glowed an even brighter greenish blue with every drop. Daphne crossed first, walking leg-deep in the river. Her splashing made the most wondrous light show in the water. And the water wasn't too deep. We followed, balancing along the tree trunk. It was a bit slippery and I almost lost footing and would have fallen had Hanna not been walking close behind and helped me across. Marcus followed last. Then we made our way up another rocky trail.

"You still like him?" I asked Hanna quietly.

She nodded.

"Then why don't you go back and talk to him?"

Hanna looked behind her. Her body shook and her arms wrapped tightly around herself. She was cold. Our casual clothes had hardly prepared us for a winter night by the Stratos. Still, the idea of talking to the boy apparently warmed her heart. She gave me a quick hug and gladly fell behind me. I hoped he'd become interested in her. I mean, it was nice that he wanted me, but my best friend was totally stricken by him.

Then I pleasantly walked alone with Daphne. The rain drizzled as I petted Daphne's head. We were standing on a rocky ledge as Hanna and Marcus walked along the path passing near the stream below.

We were getting pretty high up the mountain. I knew that, through trees and brush and beyond the river below, on a clear day, the Crystal Palace could be spotted under the mountainside. I would have loved to have shown the spectacle to Marcus, but I couldn't see anything in this storm.

"You did so good, girl," I said, petting Daphne again. "I knew you could do it."

She neighed.

"It's cold, Avva," Hanna said, catching up with Marcus behind me. Hanna yawned. "And late. The dance is probably over by now. Can't we head back to Azure Palace now?"

"See those large stones, Marcus?" I asked, pointing up a cliffside.

"Aye," Marcus said, shivering a little. "I see it."

"Those are the ramparts of Harmonia's original city. Centuries ago, from this height, Harmonia could survey any invasion below. The whole place was constructed like a fortress. If you look beyond more trees, there's even a ditch that was dug under us. It's said that stone walls were built to protect my people from invaders. I've looked and sometimes I've found rows of stone lying about the ground. I even found an ancient Mandrigelian knife here once." I pointed back to the path winding up the hill. "If we walk farther up, we'll see a single ancient structure still standing. There's only one whole structure left. It was an armory, we think, said to be a leftover structure from the original fortress. Queen Harmonia used to replenish her arms here as she warred all over the kingdom. It's the only building still standing, just a single room, really. There are more broken stone structures farther up the hillside. In war times, Harmonia didn't reside here. She spent most of her time in your lands, in a general's tent."

"Ah, Father has a general's tent."

"Harmonia's was said to have two rooms."

"Father's tent has multiple rooms. It has four rooms, and he travels with it all around the Sun Kingdom as he fights our enemies."

"Four, huh?"

"Aye. And golden goblets have been brought to King

Darius as gifts from the Northern lands. Very valuable treasures with engravings of fighters and gods from Athenia and Sparta. Even Etrurian and Phoenician, they say. You should see the reliefs on the vases. Even some golden statues of the gods. King Darius has some items dating back centuries."

"Golden, huh? He has many allies in the North?"

"No, not farther than the Isle of Napea. Few have sailed beyond your Mount Ambitus. But many of the gold items and pottery are from the North, they say. The Phoenicians trade them. They trade everything by sea to the farthest reaches of our world, or so people say."

As we turned up a flatter but narrow path in the trees, it was Marcus's turn to tell me about his lands. He continued to yap about stories of Southern Atala and the battles he had fought in only a few moons ago. He said that times were difficult, with peace being threatened by some king named Morteus. He spoke of many small skirmishes that had developed along the northern shores of Atala, part of proxy wars with Morteus's Hinterland allies. He always spit to the side when he mentioned King Morteus. He said that this king was the most horrible, vile monster in Gaia. Then he told me why. He spoke of a great war that had threatened his home when he was young. He said that, even back then, Morteus nearly burned his home and killed his mother and father. So many others were tortured or killed. I asked him about his mother. I'm not sure why I did, but I did. He said he hadn't seen his mother in over a year due to all of his father's campaigns. I said at least he knew his father. I never knew mine.

And that's when he finally did it. He held my hand.

My face burned. My palm shook a little. He squeezed it and took it up to his lips and kissed it, as if to reassure me. I didn't dare look behind me at Hanna.

Fortunately, we were almost at our destination, making our way up a last wide, muddy path. But this path was a bit slower and steeper.

The ground leveled off into a large muddy field of blue grass. I remembered running along this hilltop with Engel when I was a little girl. Of course, that had been in broad daylight, when it wasn't soaked with slushy mud and rain.

We approached a cluster of granite walls covered with red and purple moss, the remains of buildings. Roots were interwoven with the stones. I loved these structures. This was like my secret fort when I was little. I led Marcus to a single structure. A large opening in a stone wall had once been a door. Inside it was dark and dank. There were also two openings in the walls, windows once covered with glass, I guessed, now coated in moss. And the stone walls had cracks everywhere.

"Well, what do you think?" I asked smugly, leaning on the stone wall.

"It's getting very late, guys," Hanna said, yawning.

She looked tired. And . . . mad. I supposed she had just seen us holding hands.

"We should be heading back," I agreed with a nod.

"Aye," Marcus said. "I told Father I'd be home tonight after the dance. We probably should be heading back now, princess."

But then, all of a sudden, it started to pour more than ever.

The only shelter was the broken-down stone room. So we quickly ran in. But Daphne couldn't fit. She was getting drenched and shook in the cold outside, the poor thing. I ran out to help. I had to somehow get her inside the shelter. My poor unicorn kept trying to turn her head from the pelting rain.

"Avva!" cried Hanna. "Avva, come back inside!"

I cradled Daphne's head as water plummeted over my face. Then I tried again, pulling her neck toward the stone building. But she refused to duck under the arch of the stone doorway.

"Come on, Daphne!" I said. "You can't stay outside. It's raining too hard. Come on girl, come in."

She wouldn't budge. Because she wouldn't fit.

"Let me try," Marcus said.

Marcus gently grabbed Daphne by her horn, drawing her in. Marcus was strong. He helped Daphne duck her head under the granite ceiling.

Daphne neighed as she squeezed in.

"Thank you, Marcus!" I shouted, jumping into his arms. "You did it! Thank you!"

Then we just stood staring at the rain as it fell like a wall of water through the open door. Water also dripped through the cracks in the stone ceiling. But there were spots dry enough for us to avoid getting too wet.

"How could I forget?" asked Marcus. "I never showed you my gift, princess. Now would be the best time to give it to you." And he reached inside his tunic and brought out a long black stick. He waved the wand in the air. The tip flashed into a fiery torch lighting the entire room. Then he bowed before presenting it to me. "My gift for the Amazon princess. The Amazon princess of Azure Blue."

"*Some gift!*" I said with wide eyes.

"It's a torch from Henri, our court wizard," said Marcus. "A prized possession and the only magical thing I could think of that your people don't have in this wondrous land. Henri claims the light never burns out. It can keep us warm. It can be lit by waving it and doused with your palm. But, even under water, it will never go out. Only if you cup it in your hand like this."

And he cupped the fire out.

"Well, light it again, dummy!" I cried. "Quick! We're freezing."

Marcus handed it to Hanna.

"You do the honors, my lady," Marcus said, bowing before her.

The fire flashed brightly as Hanna waved it in the air. Then she touched it to a bush near a stone wall of the building. The fire illuminated the dead twigs and leaves, burning hot and bright. Then she handed the wand back to me.

"The best gift anyone's ever given us," said Hanna, clapping.

"Thank you, Marcus," I said with a nod. "I love it."

And I hugged him again.

It was still cold.

I went over to a crack in one of the stone walls and gazed at the surrounding woods. I tried to look beyond the shadowy trees in the forest, because we were at an elevation where, when the weather was clear, I knew I could spot the palace in the valley. The storm still clouded everything. Could Daphne fly through this dense fog? I shuddered. What if she couldn't? Would we have to wait until morning? And what would Mother do tonight with us missing? She would order a search party. Then, because of me, she might suspend the games!

I put my head in my hands. Then I ran wet fingers through my long, drenched hair.

"We shouldn't leave until the rain dies down, Blue," Hanna said.

"We have to," I cried, shaking my head.

"We can't," Marcus remarked morosely.

A violent crack of lightning shook the ground, and a flash of bright white light filled the room. It seemed to shake the foundations. It must have been so close as to almost strike us. Daphne jumped.

"It's all right, girl," I said, petting Daphne. "It's okay."

"Oh, Avva, I'm scared," said Hanna. "We can't fly back now. Daphne can't fly through this storm."

I put an arm around my friend. "It'll be all right."

"Oh, we should never have left, Avva," said Hanna, almost in tears. "We shouldn't have gone. We should have just stayed home."

"I know," I said, embracing her. "It'll be okay, Hanna."

"No, it won't!" And Hanna pushed me off her. "This is your fault! We're alone out here because of you! You can be so stupid! We'll have to spend the whole night in this awful place!"

"I know. I'm sorry, Hanna. I'm sorry."

"We'll make do," Marcus said with that old self-assuredness. This time, I'm not sure I minded it.

I looked down at the muddy ground. I had camped outside the palace many times before, but never in these circumstances. I had always brought a tent or at least a bag full of supplies. Was it dry enough to lie down and sleep? Stupid. This whole evening was stupid. I had been so stupid.

"Are we really going to have to stay here tonight?" asked Hanna, her whole body shaking again. "I'm scared."

"If the rain doesn't stop, I think we have to," replied Marcus.

"I'm so sorry," I said again and reached out to hug Hanna.

"I really hate you," she said, shaking her head. But then she embraced me tightly.

4

THE STORM

After dark, the sound of rain hitting the gray stones and leaves above finally calmed; the only rain dripped from the holes in the ceiling. Somehow my friends had managed to fall asleep, snoring as they leaned against Daphne. Daphne had lain down on her side on drier ground, closing her eyes too. The large opening in the stone wall was quiet and pitch black. The only light came from our fire, which still burned to my left. But I feared that soon there'd be no more kindling to burn, and we'd have only Marcus's wand. Unless the storm was over? . . . No, wind still howled outside.

I closed my eyes again and tried to rest. I thought of Marcus. He was handsome. Hanna was right about that. And he had held my hand. *MY* hand. He fancied me, not her. I wondered if my best friend would ever speak to me again when we returned. Actually, she probably wouldn't speak to me again anyway after this crazy adventure.

Mother, of course, was going to kill me. We were stuck in a storm in the middle of the night away from the castle; she'd be worried. I wondered what punishment I'd get. Onos would be worried over his son. Hanna's mother was kind; Hanna would probably spend a night without supper and that would be it. But what about me? I'm sure my wicked mother would think of something horrible to do to me.

A branch cracked outside, forcing my eyes open. I looked to my side. My friends still slept. Then I stared at the open blackness out the door. The water wasn't falling hard anymore, but the pitch-black night and the mist limited visibility to only a handful of paces outside.

Slowly and carefully I crept to the doorway to take a better look. Black and gray shadows surrounded the trees and bushes. It was still dark, but the rain was only a drizzle. That was wonderful. If the rain continued to calm, we could go home. It was so cold out. The wind blew over my cheeks and felt like ice.

Then I smelled something like mud, but it was more pungent and smelly. Like an odd gamey wild animal smell.

A shadow flew by the door. I thought it was maybe a bird, but . . . no, it was larger. I heard rustling again. I searched to my left but saw nothing. But then, gazing back into the darkness, I saw a shadow approaching. Maybe a lapis deer?

I lurched back as the animal appeared about ten paces from the shelter. Its features were shadowed, but it was bright enough to make out its silhouette. It was a humanoid, but not human, crouched down with an elongated head, unnaturally long arms, and long hands covering its knees. Its large eyes flickered in the firelight inside our shelter, and it was staring at me. I got a glimpse of its bald scalp. And I think it grimaced with large, disgusting lips. That was worse than anything else.

An amphiuma? Amphiumas were red-and-black snake-like creatures that were known to guard the entrances to Mount Ambitus. But I had never seen one. I had heard of them, in ancient myths, from Engel.

"Go away!" I snapped. "Shoo! Get out of here!"

It hissed and crept closer—too close. Now I could see its full loathsomeness.

Its black skin was wet and leathery, with bright vertical red stripes running down its diamond-shaped face. It had a fat stomach, unusually long arms, and stubby legs. Its mouth, now contorted in malice, was an ugly bright crimson with two sharp teeth.

"My home," it hissed, pointing a long fingernail at its chest. Then I turned in disgust as a black tongue the size of its face came out and brushed against one of its white eyes. "My home. *Mine.* Why you? . . . You smell nice."

And it smiled that nasty grin again.

"Who are you?"

"Ampears."

"You are an amphiuma?"

Its pungent stench surrounded me, as if I stood in a mound of freshly shoveled horse manure. And as it crept even closer, I realized with terror that it didn't walk but slithered, using its long, thick tail. When it was only a couple paces from me, I panicked and fumbled in the pocket of my pants. I carried a camping knife, dull at the center but sharp at the tip. It would have to be good enough. So I waved it in front of its face.

"Go away! Get out of here! Go away!"

It lunged at me. But that's when I forgot my friends. When those long fingers came an inch from clawing my face, it was hurled inside the room. I lost my balance from fright and fell to my side. Then I saw my rescuer. Daphne squealed, slamming the creature with a mighty feathered wing. She repeatedly slammed her entire body into the small creature, as if smashing a bug. The amphiuma, only half my height, was thrown over and over against the stone walls, so hard as to almost burst through the foundation. Then Marcus came from behind me and lunged at the creature with a knife of his own. Marcus didn't have to help. Daphne, who, ever since I was a child, I had thought of as merely my cute pet, became the most violent animal I had ever seen. She mercilessly mauled the creature, tossing it about the room until it was finally thrown outside. And my unicorn's attack didn't stop there. However hard it had been to get Daphne inside, she smashed against the walls, over and over, until she freed herself from the doorway.

She charged the creature outside. Then the amphiuma screamed as it was pummeled again. Daphne chased the monster, disappearing into the shadowy woods.

"Are you all right, Avva?" asked Marcus, over me, panting. Now the boy looked like a real soldier. He carried his knife in one hand and was crouched in a battle pose ready to strike.

"Yes . . . yes, I think I'm fine, Marcus."

"We have to get out of here," said Hanna. "I hear they come in packs. Are you sure you're okay, Blue?"

No. I felt faint and sick. The stone walls were spinning. And I couldn't get the image out of my mind of that beast's claws an inch from my face.

"We have to leave," Marcus echoed, catching his breath and nodding.

"We'll leave when Daphne gets back," I said, out of breath too. "Through the darkness. Storm or not. We'll fly away from here somehow."

Marcus nodded. Then he searched outside the door.

"I don't see her," said Marcus. "Or hear her. Where'd she go? I can barely see anything. It might not be raining, but the fog is so thick."

He returned to the shelter and reached out a hand to assist Hanna while helping me up.

"A remarkable horse, indeed, princess," Marcus said. Then he shook his head vehemently. "You win. That horse is indeed the fiercest animal I've ever seen, hardly lame." He smiled. Then he gasped another breath. "A remarkable horse. The most remarkable animal I've ever known. How old did you say that horse is?"

"Some victory," I said, shaking my head. "I don't care."

Then I took another deep breath. And then I thought I'd cry.

But instead I worried. If Daphne had merely been chasing the creature, she should have been back by now.

That's when we heard the most terrible sound. Having tended Daphne ever since I could walk, I knew every snort, grunt, or neigh that beautiful girl was capable of emitting from her wonderful lips—every sound and every call. I knew when she was hungry or when she was thirsty. Tired or distressed. But once, after running through wheat fields and falling in a ditch, she broke her leg. I heard this same shrieking howl now. It was an unsettling call of pain. And with that, I knew Daphne was in peril.

I went crazy. I forgot everything, my friends, any danger, and ran headlong into the night, running wildly over bushes and around trees toward her yelps. I lost all my senses, running for the longest time in darkness, occasionally twisting my boot among rocks or sliding on puddles alongside the wet marsh. Then I started climbing down a muddy incline covered in thrush, away from any trail, toward her screams. I didn't care. I had to find her!

Finally, I caught her shadow rising in the air up above the trees and then violently crashing back down. She would hover in the air for a moment and then be hurled to the ground. Marcus and Hanna kept yelling from behind. I think I heard them climbing down the muddy hillside too. And then, as if to make everything worse, it started to rain again.

As I clambered through shrubs, I finally spotted Daphne trapped in a hole. She was surrounded by a large group of the vile monsters. I wasn't sure what the red-and-black snakes were doing until they started jabbing my poor pet with long wooden spears. It reminded me of our Court chefs skewering meat. Watching those sharp sticks hit my beloved unicorn was the worst thing I'd ever experienced. And it was then that I guessed at the vipers' sinister intentions. Perhaps they weren't only fighting my pet for revenge. Perhaps the snakes intended to feast on her!

Either Marcus or Hanna grabbed me. I didn't know, I didn't care. I threw whoever it was off.

"*Stop, Avva!*" cried Hanna. "*Stop! Stay away from them!*"

"*Avva, come back!*" cried Marcus.

The rain began to pour.

"*Daphne!*" I cried in madness. "*Daphne! We have to help her!*"

I forced my eyes open in the pelting rain. And in the downpour, I shook my long wet hair back and caught glimpses of her wings and body rising again. She crashed back down into the muddy hole.

"*Avva!*"

Someone grabbed me again. Instinctively, using all my training from Cambria, I knelt down and tried to throw whoever held me. But my assailant was skilled. As I shifted my weight, the person switched theirs. Finally, I saw his face. This wasn't an amphiuma, it was Marcus. But I didn't care. He was preventing me from rushing down into the ditch with the creatures and saving Daphne.

Then I heard another terrible cry from Daphne!

"Let me go!" I cried. "Let me go, Marcus! I have to help her! They're killing her!"

I fought Marcus's clutches to break free. Hanna slid beside the two of us trying to stop me too.

"*Let me go! They're gonna kill her, guys! Let me go!*"

"*Leave her, Avva!*" cried Marcus, pulling me back. "*There's too many of them! It's too late.*"

That did it. It was wet enough for me to slide from his hands. I threw him over my side. Hanna tried to grab me too, but I shook her off easily. Then I leaped into the ditch, sliding down a steep, muddy wall.

Daphne had stopped moving at the bottom. And all the amphiumas had disappeared.

My poor unicorn struggled to breathe as she lay in the

large muddy ditch. Every move I made slapped water against the mud. The hole was filling with water. Beside her, I could see dark spots along her flank. It was too dark to see the spots properly, but no doubt it was blood.

She turned her head and winced. So I hugged her and cried.

"Oh Daphne! Daphne, what have they done to you!"

"We have to leave, Avva!" cried Hanna. *"Get out of there!"*

Daphne lifted her head weakly in my embrace. I could see the pain in her eyes. She snorted, struggling to breathe.

"What have they done to you, girl? How could they?"

I ran my hand along her soft, wet mane. It seemed to comfort her, but her breathing was labored. I snuggled her. Then I looked down at the wound on her side, but it was too dark to discern how bad it was. She struggled and tried to rise but then fell back and closed her eyes.

Then she stopped moving altogether.

Daphne had died. Daphne—the legendary royal unicorn that had once been the companion of my grandmother, Queen Dainya—the legendary monokera of Colchis, was dead. A hero to my people. Fighter of the dragon. Daphne, my pet and my beloved companion, who I had known and cared for all my life, was now dead.

I felt the cold wind and icy rain. I hadn't even noticed how cold it was. And then I heard Hanna sobbing above the ditch too.

Of course, it was my fault. All of this was my fault. I should never have taken her here. Hanna had been right, Daphne *was* old. If she hadn't been injured, or lame, as Marcus had called her, she probably could have fought off this whole group of creatures.

Between sobs, I heard scurrying in the bushes above. I looked up, and my companions were gone! Marcus shouted. It was another struggle. This time, the monsters were attacking my friends!

I rushed to the wall, but it was slimy and hard to climb over.

I heard Hanna scream.

I caught the white eyes of those terrible creatures in the darkness at the top of the ditch. That's when I fell into a rage. All I had was my camping knife, but it didn't matter. It had a sharp end and that would have to do. With all my might, I dug my knife into the mud and clawed with my fingers, trying to climb out of the ditch. Then, as I gazed up at two hideous grinning lips, I realized that this ditch had been laid as a trap. These creatures were not so stupid after all. Maybe they weren't hunting the unicorn. Maybe they were hunting me?

Every shout of my companions made me more determined. So I climbed, grabbing the mud with the edge of my knife or with my fingernails. Climbing was a skill I had learned, and I knew how to scale walls. I used all my training to get out of their trap—not just to free myself, but to help my friends.

When I was at the top, I lodged my knife in the hand of a creature crouching over me. The beast screamed. Then I grabbed it by its other arm and threw it over my back into the ditch. The other one faced me. I wrestled it and then stuck my camping knife, sharp at the tip, right into its back.

The mist was rising and I found that, in my frenzy, I had slid down the entire mountainside. The shore of the Stratos River was right beside us now. Rays of green sunlight rose over the blue-green forest, and I was shocked to see how many of these horrible snake-men, these *things*, surrounded us.

I leaped on another. I had to. Marcus was fighting two others with his dagger, farther down near the water. Hanna was using her bare hands, wrestling another. I had always felt like my friend's grappling skills were shoddy, but when it came to a matter of survival, somehow everything Hanna had learned from our great General Cambria came to fruition and led her to savagely suffocate one of the miserable snakes. We were killing them. But there were many more descending the mountain from the trees.

My fury changed to a fight for survival. My dull knife was useless. I could stab straight, but it was so blunt on the edge. So I, like Hanna, had to choke some of the slippery snakes to death. But when even more monsters came out from the woods, I lost hope. There were too many of them.

That's when I heard whistling. At first, I thought it was the wind stirring up twigs and branches. Soon I knew better. A couple monsters who were about to finish off Hanna fell over her body, struck dead. Then two of the beasts flew off Marcus's back, tripped, and fell into the river, never to rise from the glowing waters again. I rolled with another on my back. It reached down to bite me with its long fangs, but it, too, fell from my body after a windy "whoosh" sound. Then I heard screams. This time, it wasn't us—it was all the vermin running for their lives. Some fled into the river; others climbed back up into the woods.

I got up from my side, looking around me. There must have been ten bodies lying dead around the river shore. And the mist had completely lifted. The rain had calmed to a drizzle. And the shiny, glowing blue water of the Stratos flowed by me.

Near a bunch of blue trees along the river, I saw our hero in the air. Cambria flew proudly atop her great brown unicorn, Ranun, still hunting, throwing volley after volley of arrows in every direction. She kept shooting, never missing, emptying the quiver on her back. It was mechanical and methodical, but as graceful as a dancer. When finished, she leaped from her unicorn near us and pulled out her sword, running through any beast stupid enough to still face her. Her swordplay was like a dance too, so skilled it looked more like a bother to her than a fight for survival.

Cambria's scarlet armor shone as the morning rays hit the valley. As she stood crouched in a fighting position, searching for more to kill, Hanna ran into her arms. I did too.

"I'm so glad I found you, children," Cambria said. "By the gods, we searched everywhere."

Hanna cried in her arms while Cambria gently ran her hands over our heads. Then she patted Hanna's back, grabbed a blanket in a satchel hung over Ranun's side, and draped it over us. Hanna still stared at the ground, crying. Marcus and I just searched the trees, as if still expecting another attack.

"And how are you, my brave soldier?" Cambria asked Marcus.

"Fine," he said.

I didn't think he was fine.

Cambria looked at the fallen creatures lying on the ground around us and shook her head. "Seems you had quite a fight. Let me look at all of you. Is anyone wounded?"

There were cuts. Hanna had a gash on her arm. It was a bite from those horrible fangs. I had two bites on my leg. But Marcus had endured the worst of it. A wound in his side was bleeding. She led him by the shoulder over to Ranun and grabbed further supplies from her bag. Then she wrapped his stomach tightly.

"I kept telling myself that I'd punish you," Cambria said, "but I think you've had punishment enough, princess." She looked at the bodies of the amphiumas on the ground again. "Seems Diana and I will need to return and lay down some more mouse traps."

"You are the queen's chief general, right?" asked Marcus. "I remember you from the opening ceremony." He stood tall all of a sudden, acting all sure of himself again.

"Cambria," she said with a nod, touching her breastplate. "I am the general of the Amazons, like your father is the general of the Sun Kingdom. But my least favorite job is to go searching in the middle of the night during a rainstorm for naughty children who've strayed into Ambitus Forest." She smiled gently at his annoyed expression and hit him on his back. "Never mind. I also enjoy a bit of amphiuma hunting, I suppose."

But then my happiness at seeing Cambria left me. I thought of Daphne.

Cambria seemed to notice and came over.

"What's the matter, princess?"

"Daphne."

"Daphne," Cambria said with a nod. "What about her?" She quickly scanned the trees. "Where did she go?"

"She didn't make it."

"What do you mean she didn't make it! Where is Queen Dainya's unicorn, Avva?"

I led her to the ditch. Or . . . those beasts' trap. Cambria was as upset as I had been at the sight of my fallen unicorn. She slid down the ditch and fell on her knees. Tears ran from her eyes. She held the unicorn's head in her arms and nuzzled her, as I had. And she stayed down there for what seemed like an eternity. It made me and Hanna cry all over again.

Then Cambria slowly rose and reached her arms up for us to help her. We helped her climb out of the muddy ditch.

"All will be better," Cambria said, forcing a smile. "Let's get back to Azure Palace. You three can catch a cold in this storm."

5

MOTHER

Mother sat atop her dais, wearing the same long black cloth covering her hair and formal purple striped dress she had worn at the greeting of King Darius. I still wore a simple brown tunic. I suppose that was a little rebellious. She had invited me as my queen, not as my mother, and I was wearing simple everyday clothes.

I was a little upset at her for not greeting me like the rest of the Court did when we returned. Everyone else hugged and kissed us, so happy that we returned safe. Poor Engel fell apart in my arms. Even the king visited us and was happy for my safety. Not Mother. No, not Queen Delia. She had avoided me all day, finally summoning me here tonight, as if I were one of her guest subjects.

I walked down the central aisle of the Court, approaching the throne.

Engel looked grave, sitting on the first marble step under Mother, looking down. He was the only other one in the room except Cambria, who stood guard at the entry doors on the far side of the Great Hall.

Mother didn't smile. She just raised a crystal glass of red myrle berry wine and sipped it.

I bowed deeply before her.

"Avivae, I only have one thing to ask you and then—" She waved dismissively, seeming to have difficulty controlling herself. "I would prefer you not speak to me again the rest of the night."

"Yes, Mother?"

"Address me as your queen."

"Yes, Queen Delia?"

There was something about my tone that made Engel open his eyes and quickly shake his head.

"Why did you take Daphne out of her stable?"

"I was . . . an idiot."

"That doesn't answer my question."

"I love Daphne more than anyone. You know I've groomed her and cared for her every day for years. There is no one who is sadder about what happened than—"

"I asked you a question and you have yet to answer me."

I thought for a moment. This was tricky. If I told her about the stupid fight with Marcus, I might endanger Marcus even more. Not only that, but the reason was idiotic and likely would only anger her more. Then again, she probably was using her guile and already knew full well why I had taken the prized unicorn out of the towers. She just wanted to lecture me until my face turned purple. Or I lost control of myself and sobbed. It would hardly be the first time.

She sipped more wine and gave me another fake smile. I knew inside she wanted to charge at me and impale me with the royal scepter.

"I felt like it was stuffy in the Court," I said, throwing my long hair back, "and I wanted to get out, away from all the festivities. I wanted to be alone, so I took the unicorn and flew around the palace for a while. Then I saw Hanna with Marcus, you know, the general's son, down near the drawbridge, so I thought I'd join them." Mother kept drinking her wine, but she was losing her fake smile. She started to blush a little. "Marcus was so impressed by the unicorn that he asked if he could mount her. I told him Daphne was such a magnificent unicorn that he could mount her only if he flew with me and Hanna. So I got them to ride a little around the palace. That's all. Then the tempest arose, and I was forced by the wind to turn to the great Mount."

I stopped. Because Mother had put her hand over her eyes and was shaking her head.

"We . . . strayed in the bad weather. The rain blinded me, and I had to land far from the palace, near the Stratos."

"Why does she do this, Engel?" she asked, looking down at the dwarf.

"Avivae loved Daphne dearly," Engel said. "I think, Your Majesty, that Avva is grieving, perhaps more than any of us, over the loss of her unicorn."

"*She is not!*" Mother shouted, her voice echoing in the Hall. She jumped up in rage and pounded the arm of her chair. "*She cannot! She does not know how much the entire kingdom mourns from this outrage! You, princess, may miss your dear pet, but our people miss their hero! Daphne, the monokera who protected us, fought the dragon, and guarded your grandmother in Colchis, was a symbol for our people! Not only did your grandmother fight the dragon, she fought Olympus itself with that steed!*" She wagged her finger at me and, for a moment, I expected her to descend the steps and finally slug me. "You may have lost your pet, you stupid little girl, but the kingdom lost a hero!"

It was too much for me. I didn't care about her raging. But talking about Daphne dying brought me to tears. I fell down on my knees and cried.

Engel got up and hobbled toward me.

"*Stay away from her, Engel!*" yelled Delia. "*Stay away! We all spoil her!*"

Engel bowed deeply before his queen and stepped back.

"I know, Mother! I know! She saved me that night.

Daphne rescued all of us. I know what I did and it was wrong. I didn't mean–"

"And yet you stand here and lie to me? You stand before the queen of Azure, the Amazon queen of Napea, and lie to her face?"

"I didn't lie." I looked up, brushing off tears. "I didn't."

"You did. I have already spoken with Marcus. I got most of the story from him. Then I got the rest from Hanna's mother. You took a prized unicorn of my people, too old to even ride, a symbol for every nymph, and flew her leagues to the Stratos. *For what!* A bet? You wanted to protect your pride over the words of the general's son. Do you deny this? Is that not what happened, Avivae Ambrosia?"

"I don't," I said. I met her gaze. "I mean . . . I did. Yes. That is what happened, Mother."

"His words, Avivae? The whole reason for this tragedy was a boy's insult? It's your pride! Why didn't you honestly tell me it was for a princess's stupid pride?"

"I . . . well, you knew it . . . anyway. But I didn't want to hurt Marcus or Hanna."

"You act like a little toddler. And now, after you have endangered Hanna's and Marcus's lives, you dare claim to protect them?"

I looked away toward the walls of the Court. It was dark outside. The beautiful palace gardens were shadowed by the coming evening. Still the silhouettes of the roses and shrubs were beautiful. It would have been very beautiful, had I not felt so miserable.

"What is it you want from me?" I asked, clenching my teeth, still staring out the black window.

"No, Avva," warned Engel. "No."

I turned back and glared at her. For a moment, even my brave mother leaned back in her chair in surprise.

"You called me here to fight?" I cried. "What's the point if you already knew the whole story? Maybe, if you were a *real* mother, you would have come to me when I returned and hugged me, being happy for my return, happy that I was still alive."

"*How dare you!*"

She threw her crystal wine glass at me. It landed a foot away, but the intent was clear. It nearly clocked Engel in the head before shattering on the floor. Then she looked down at the broken glass by my feet in disgust.

"My queen, if I may speak," Engel said softly.

"*You may not!*"

My mother and I stared into each other's eyes. Cambria rushed halfway down the Hall to try to do something. What, I don't know. I don't think it was to arrest me.

"My queen," Engel said, "Delia, if I may speak, Avivae is—"

"Shut your mouth, Engel," she said, still staring at me. "You may not speak."

I looked down.

"Dearest *daughter*," she spat, finally looking away. But she emphasized the word *daughter* in disgust. "My *daughter*, you endangered the lives of your best friend and General Onos's only son, hardly the act of an Amazon princess, or of a daughter of mine. Then, in the midst of it all, *daughter of mine*, you destroyed the happiness the games had brought to the Court with your disappearance. Everyone in Azure Palace who had joyfully looked forward to the games today lost everything over their concern for you and your foolish friends' welfare, all for your pride and an idiotic bet. Your actions are reprehensible, and I find it difficult to decide on a punishment strong enough to fit your crime."

She slapped the arm of her throne again and gazed at the dark windows, just like I had. We both did. I caught Engel looking at me, worried. Still, he didn't dare approach. He sat back down under Mother.

Cambria slowly headed back to her post by the door.

"I can't bring myself to do what Onos did to his son, Engel," she said after an exasperated sigh. Then she forced her disingenuous grin at me again. "It was cruel. His punishment was painful, but quick. Yours, *daughter*, will be long and hard. Hear my edict. Engel, write down my law.

"Princess Avivae Ambrosia. You shall atone for one year. During that year, you will have no access to any unicorn. You shall have no entrance to the tower stables, no flights, no unicorn to tend to on your own. Tending the stables is what you love the most, and that is what you will forfeit. I was going to give you a unicorn of your own upon the coming year. Not anymore. Now you won't have one. You will only train with Cambria and study with Engel. You will answer to me regarding all your free time. Every moment will be under my watch and only by my consent. You will not go off on your own under any circumstances. This is your punishment. The loss of your freedom."

Then she leaned back and glared at me.

"I accept."

"*You accept?*" she asked with a laugh. "You *accept?* How droll, you arrogant little witch. What gives you any right, my spoiled brat, to do anything else?"

I just nodded.

Engel brushed back a tear from his eye. I wondered if he cried for me or if he, too, hated me for what had happened to our beloved unicorn.

"May I go, Mother?"

"Oh, yes, Avivae," she said, waving her hand at me. "Please go away."

I bowed sadly and walked down the aisle. I caught Cambria looking at me by the doors. She bowed.

"For the rest of the games," the queen hollered across the Hall, "you will be present at every dance and ceremony. There is a dance tomorrow night. Wear your best clothes. Then, in two days, we shall have our games. The games which you have forced me to delay by two days for an entire kingdom."

"I will be there, Queen Delia," I said formally, turning with a quick bow.

Cambria put a hand on my shoulder. But even she didn't dare say anything.

"I am pleased, Avivae, that you have returned safe," Mother added as I approached the hallway. It was a bit too late, said with my back turned as the great wooden doors closed.

6

THE DANCE

The next night was a reprieve from all the doom and gloom. I think the dark mood in the Court had been a greater punishment than my mother's rules. So many people seemed to glare at me in suspicion after our return. I think they were so scared I'd do something stupid again to further stall the games. But that night, once again, nymphs were making their faces pretty, trying on their best dresses, or rushing past shops along our main street and over the drawbridge to meet more men. And then they arrived at our evening dance.

Dance had been such an important thing for my people since before the days of Harmonia. An Amazon nymph was taught how to dance with just as much focus as she was taught how to wield a sword. And, in many ways, the technique of the Amazon warrior was to combine the grace of movement in our dance with the deadliness of the sword.

All my people were so excited.

I wasn't. Daphne had been my confidant, my dearest friend. And now she was dead. I couldn't stop thinking of her. Any punishment Mother ordained was nothing compared to losing my beloved unicorn.

Now Hanna accompanied me over our great wooden drawbridge, with so many people crowding us that I worried the old drawbridge would break. Then we followed the excited mob under torchlight over our purple fields, past many red tents, and toward the main amphitheater. Eva walked with us. My two friends were so excited watching all the boys nearby. Hundreds of men would be at the dance, just as there had been at the last dance, which I had been avoiding in the stable tower.

Would Marcus be there?

"Oh, Avva, aren't you excited?" Eva asked, wide-eyed. She was a tall nymph, about a year younger than me. "Who will you dance with tonight, princess?"

"I don't know," I said with a shrug. "Maybe Marcus."

Eva giggled. Hanna turned sour.

"Oh, stop it, Hanna," I said, touching her back. "You know he may not even be there. Mother said he was severely punished. Have you thought that the general might not let him go tonight?"

"I'm not going to the dance just to see Marcus, Avva," Hanna said. "Why should I care?"

But she did care. Quite obviously.

When we stood in line at the entrance to a huge tent, Hanna got real close to me, whispering so Eva couldn't hear. Eva was oblivious anyway, staring at all the men.

"Avva," Hanna said very quietly, "just tell me. Tell me the truth, okay? Do you fancy him?"

"Who?"

"Don't be stupid," Hanna said in a hushed whisper. "You know who. I saw you holding hands. I saw it that night in—" She couldn't bring herself to say *Ambitus Forest*. Neither of us wanted to talk about it. I didn't think we'd want to talk about it again for a very long time.

"It just happened," I replied. "He was getting emotional about the war and his concern about this King Morteus fellow threatening him and his family. He got me feeling sorry for him. That's all. It was nothing."

Eva had a big smile now, but she was still acting like she was paying attention to strangers around us.

"Oh, Hanna, he's an idiot," I added. "Just forget him. He's an idiot."

"I think he's wonderful. He risked his life to save us. He was like our sentry. I don't think he's an idiot at all. I think he's strong and nice and so handsome. You saw how he fought with his knife. He protected us. He's brave and . . ."

"Gallant?" I giggled. She joined me, laughing.

"Well, we'll see if he even shows up," I said. The line was finally moving into the grand tent. Looking over the shoulders of the people ahead of us, I saw even brighter firelight through the red cloth of the tent walls. "He's in a lot of trouble with Onos. Mother hinted that the general did something terrible to him. Something quick, she said. I just hope he didn't hurt him."

"Can you . . . well, can you not dance with him tonight?"

Hmm. I hadn't thought of that. As much as he annoyed me, he was cute. I thought I'd like to dance with him. But then I thought of my best friend. I touched her arm and said, "Okay, I won't."

"Thank you, princess!" Hanna said with a large grin. "Thank you! But . . . do you think he's cute?"

"Oh, Hanna! Shut it."

"I think he is," Eva said, leaning toward us with a big grin.

We entered the reception hall. The tent could probably fit a few hundred—and it'd have to. Most men were already eating or drinking. The men looked so formal. Their long hair and beards were nicely combed or tied, their tunics were fresh and brightly clean, and their pants were pressed. Even their brown leather boots were polished. Many men drank beer, wine, and mead, shouting and acting crazy, engaging in raucous banter. A great many bowed to me, recognizing me, as we passed. They hadn't been nice to me yesterday after we had returned from the Stratos and mother had threatened to cancel the games.

Iris ran up and gave me a great big hug. I ran my hand through her long red hair—so rare a color for a nymph, but so beautiful. Today her hair was brushed to one side. Then she led us to a large table she and some of my other friends had claimed. Debra and Ailla were already leaning on their sides on pillows by the table. They were dressed elegantly and smelled nice too. We all commented on their pretty dresses and tied curls. Then we nudged each other, looking over at the boys. The boys would smile or wave, staring at us, acting all suave, and my friends would stupidly giggle or turn away.

Then we ate. The food was delicious. Some of the cakes had been prepared by me in the kitchen with our chefs. There was pheasant, perfectly spiced and browned, plates of grapes and olives, mutton, beef, delightful cheeses, pies, and, well, all sorts of yummy things. I didn't sit on a chair, as was customary for a nymph, but lay on my side per the men's custom. Their custom had certainly saved Mother's carpenters a lot of work making hundreds of chairs, I suppose. Many older men and women sat close together. And I saw a few couples leave the reception to go out into the night for a stroll.

Then I saw Mother. She wore another long violet dress with a collar, this one an even darker purple. Her long black hair was combed nicely. We looked like twins, unintentionally, wearing dresses of similar colors. Among Amazon nymphs, it wasn't uncommon for daughters to be mistaken for mothers, for a nymph never ages after twenty or thirty. We were immortally young, unless mortally wounded in combat.

Mother walked by each table. When she reached ours, she waved discreetly but made every effort to turn her back on me. She was very kind to my friends though, even Hanna. Beside her was King Darius, looking twice her size, mainly in girth not stature. He wore the most ordinary tunic, hardly kingly. But his black beard and long hair were perfectly combed. I was surprised when he bowed before me. He gazed at me with those sharp, intense black eyes.

I stood up with my friends and bowed before him.

"My lady," he said, reaching for my hand and kissing the back of it. "Princess, you look radiant. I trust you shall honor the king with a dance tonight?"

"Of course, King Darius," I said with a giggle. "It would be my honor."

"Ahh, you warm my heart, Princess Anne."

And indeed, it seemed I did. He seemed so fond of me.

"Come, Darius," said my mother, "leave Avivae with her friends."

"I'm glad you're safe now, princess," he said. "You gave us all such a fright."

"You already said as much the other day, Your Majesty," I said with a chuckle. "But thanks again."

"Aye, one dance, princess. One. And tomorrow, I've arranged for us to sit together at the games, if you would like?"

"I'd be honored, sir."

Then he placed an arm around my mother, kissed her cheek, and moved to the next table.

Hanna and Iris completely lost control of themselves. They were practically rolling on the floor in laughter over my conversation with the king.

"What?" I asked.

"Aren't you a little young?" asked Hanna. Iris laughed some more.

"Don't be stupid."

"Is that why you haven't been fancying any of the boys?" asked Iris, her light gray eyes bulging in dumb mirth. "*I would like just one dance with you, princess,*" she mocked.

"Quiet," I said dismissively. But I felt myself blush.

"But . . . I suppose the king did ask *me* for a dance, didn't he?"

Everyone roared with laughter.

I couldn't find Marcus in the tents during the dinner reception. I looked—not as much as Hanna, but I looked.

After bells rang we were ushered outside to the outdoor stadium again. Tonight the stadium had been lit up with a thousand torches.

Making our way in another queue, I spotted Marcus standing in center field, by a torch on a pole, in the same formal dress as the other men. Somehow it looked funny on him. He had this frilly white cloth about his neck, which matched the frilliness of his long white peplos, which reached his ankles. It made his skin appear the darkest shade of black. It looked absolutely ridiculous, and I had to turn away. But then seeing Hanna still ogling him was too much—I couldn't stop myself from bursting out laughing. General Onos looked regal in a long brown robe and the fur of a lion about his neck. His chest showed through, and I marveled at the musculature of that man. Other boys were looking over at my friends. A really cute tall pale boy, drinking from a wooden cup, was among them. No, he wasn't staring at my friends; he was looking at *me*, it seemed. The boy was named Felix and, according to Hanna, he was Andalay's boyfriend. Hanna had told me all about this boy and how Andalay had cared for him after he was shipwrecked a couple years ago. But I'm not sure Hanna's gossip was correct. Andalay was nowhere in sight.

Felix was wearing a very formal light green tunic over brown pants. He wore a golden necklace, and his hair was slicked back. His only problem was his face. His forehead had blemishes. Well, no one's perfect. I found him really cute, cuter than Marcus, really.

And he kept looking at me.

Dead center in the dusty dark-blue field sat a small person on a very small wooden chair. It was none other than my favorite purple dwarf, Engel. Engel sat strumming his fingers over a lyre, projecting his voice and singing to everyone. Engel had sung to me ever since I was a baby and frequently entertained my mother, but somehow I hadn't expected him to sing tonight. Why not? His voice was amazing.

In front of him danced many nymphs wearing tight light-blue and green clothing, so translucent as to reveal a bit too much of their bodies underneath. Many danced with saffron and turquoise streamers; others provided Engel with percussion accompaniment with hand drums. It is said that Mandrigel dwarfs are the best bards in all of Gaia. Indeed, Engel, the last of the Mandrigel, had the best voice I'd ever heard. The mix of music and dance on the stage, in the flickering firelight, was magical.

Many nymphs walked with their lovers or sat upon our newly constructed wooden benches, simply watching. Hanna and I didn't. We walked straight toward the dance platform near center field. Marcus was looking uncomfortable in the torchlight beside his large father. When the general saw us, he turned and bowed to me.

"Ah, princess," General Onos said with a smile. "I was so happy to hear you're all right."

I bowed before the general. Then I turned to Marcus.

"Hi, Marcus," I said.

"I think, if it hadn't been for all the heroics of my son," General Onos said, "I would have skinned this lad alive. But he told me how he protected you, and that was enough for me to give him a lighter sentence."

"*Protected me!?*" I snapped. I looked over at Marcus. He quickly looked away. "But sir, no man protects——"

"Forget it, Avva," Hanna said in a hushed voice, staring at Marcus. And then she squeezed my arm tightly, almost hurting me.

"It's good to see you again, Avva," Marcus interrupted.

He bowed before me and gave me a quick hug. Then he hugged Hanna.

"You too, Marcus," Hanna said quietly, her blue face turning a shade of red.

"I suppose you three have some catching up to do," General Onos said, hitting his son hard on the back. "Go spend some time with your friends, son. Tonight, enjoy yourself, for tomorrow, my lad, in the games, you will compete and provide honor to me. Then we will return home, and you will atone for putting your friends in danger."

"Yes, Father," he said, looking down. He seemed depressed.

I couldn't believe it. The nerve of him! *Protected me?* This boy was so full of himself. How dare he tell his father that. If I had his knife, I'd sure protect him right now. I considered taking Hanna's hand and heading back to our friends, but then I saw her eyes. They were looking dreamily at the idiot.

The general left just in time. As massive and mighty as the man was, he didn't strike me as much of a graceful dancer, and with the next song by Engel being so romantic and lovely, everyone danced with their arms around one another.

Marcus put a hand out to dance with me. I tried to ignore him and glanced at Hanna, but, as usual, the cocky boy would not relent.

"Go ahead," Hanna whispered in my ear.

So then we were dancing. Marcus and I. Because *I* wanted to? Or because *he* did? I was in the arms of the man who I owed my life to? Because *he protected me?* Really? Well, he sure was a clumsy dancer, I'll tell you that.

"How dare you," I snarled in his ear.

"What?"

"How dare you tell your father you protected me? That you *saved* me? That is ridiculous."

"Oh, that. Well, Avva, if you remember, I did watch over you two that night while you slept."

"You fell asleep."

I had to pull him a little to the left to avoid stomping on an older couple's feet. Far back in the seats I spotted Mother again. She seemed to not be scowling at me anymore. Perhaps, she wasn't so angry.

"We all fell asleep, Avva. Look, can we talk about something else?"

"You didn't rescue anyone. You lied to him."

"Must we fight?" he asked, looking into my eyes. "Fine, I lied. Is that better?"

"Daphne rescued us. She died for us, Marcus."

"Avva, if I hadn't told Father that I rescued you two, he would have whipped me good."

From his eyes, I believed him. I leaned my head into his shoulder. "You can be so annoying."

But we still swayed back and forth to the music.

Then Engel stopped singing, and only the percussion of the dancers and the beautiful music of lyres echoed throughout the camp.

"You smell nice," he said.

Ooohh, shut up.

"Well, I must say, in those clothes you look ridiculous."

That was cruel, but he laughed. "Father made me wear it."

"I didn't see you this morning," I said. "Where've you been?"

"Father won't let me out. If it weren't for the festival, I'd be in a lot more trouble."

"Same with me. Mother will probably not let me leave the palace for many moons after our adventure."

"Look, Avva, I'm sorry. You're right. I didn't protect you . . . I saw the way you fought, you didn't need me. But, you see, back in Azerban, a lady cares for the house. She cooks and cleans and mends our clothes. None would ever touch a sword. I'm not accustomed to women fighting, like you."

"Sounds like you enslave your women."

"I suppose an Amazon would think that."

I was surprised suddenly by a tap on my shoulder. Marcus and I stopped and I turned. It was King Darius, jovial as always, with a large grin. He held his hand out to me.

"Young man, would you do me the honor of lending me the hand of the princess?"

Marcus nodded and let go of me. Coincidentally, at that very moment Hanna happened to be just a couple paces away from Marcus. *Coincidentally*. She looked at him. My friend was so pretty. I wished he would just go after her instead.

Well, he did. He reached out to her, asking her to dance.

The music did not speed up. It was still soft and melodic.

The king was such a huge man. Not in height—for we nymphs are tall, and I had grown almost to my full height—but broad. His great coat was decorated with a heavy leopard pelt, and I felt it brush along my face as I leaned on his huge chest.

"Are you having a good time, princess?"

"The festival's a nice change. Normally, this time of year, I would be busy in the fields gathering food before the winter snow."

"A princess? Working in the fields?"

"All Napeans work with our subjects."

"I admire your people's ways."

"But we are different."

"You are very different. And I love that as well."

I glanced up at his face. The king had such a jovial smile. That was the thing about this king: he was always so happy. He seemed to be the complete opposite of my mother.

"How much longer will you be staying here?" I asked.

"Are you so eager to get rid of me?"

"Of course not."

"The games shall be only a half fortnight by your mother's decree. Believe me, I'd rather stay longer."

"Why don't you? You know, I've never seen my mother so happy."

I had guessed that they were in love. No one admitted to it, but it was obvious. So I couldn't understand why he had to leave. Then his expression changed. That joy that he carried everywhere left him for a moment, and he looked terribly sad.

"My dear girl, I would give anything in the world to stay here longer."

"Then why don't you?"

We had to stop for a moment.

The music changed and Engel began to sing again.

"Come with me for a moment," he said.

The king gently took me by the arm and led me through the other dancers and across the field to the darker, quieter section of the stadium. As we stood in the shadow of one of the only torchlit poles, I caught Mother staring at us for some reason.

"Avva," he said, taking my hand. "I can't stay with your mother. It is forbidden. Do you know this?"

"I know men can come only during the games. But you are a king. I can't see why you can't stay longer if you decree it."

He placed a hand on my shoulder. "No man is allowed here. It is by no law of a king or queen, princess, but of the gods. In fact, if it weren't for your disappearance, we would have been gone in only a few more days."

"I know."

He nodded quickly, then he looked at my mother making her way across the field. For a moment, he squinted angrily. What was going on? And why was Mother walking over?

"It's a hard world, child."

"I'm not a child."

It was a stupid thing to say, but he seemed to lighten up as he turned back to me.

"No, you're not. You are a lady. We all hold so many secrets in life. Some held until we fall to Elysium. Lies seem to accumulate, Anna. Many, if we unveil them, can damage friends, family, or reputation. You must know that I love your mother dearly, more than anyone in the world." He paused for a moment and a sly smile ran over his face. "Perhaps not more than anyone."

"What are you trying to say, King Darius?"

He stopped. I noticed a couple kissing not far from us in the shadows. And another boy was just standing by his lonesome squinting at all the entertainment in center field.

"Have you been to Azerban?" he asked, leaning against a wooden column.

"No. It's forbidden to step foot in your yellow lands."

"I think you'd find it beautiful. Perhaps not as beautiful as here, but very beautiful. My kingdom, Castle Cove, is very beautiful. There is nothing more beautiful than Azure Blue, but I'd love it if one day you should see my home too. Now that you and your mother have shown me yours. It would be my pleasure."

And then I thought I understood why he was confiding in me. He probably intended to marry my mother. That was it. That was what all this was about. Perhaps Mother didn't want me to know yet?

But by marrying, they could bring great peace between Azurea and Atala. Well, there already was peace due to their fondness, I supposed.

But. . . if he married her. . . maybe he could be the father I never had. He could be *my* father.

"I would love to see your castle," I blurted joyfully. "But, you know, we're not allowed to cross the Strait according to the edict."

"I know, Anna, I know that very well. Believe me."

I leaned back against a wooden plank in the shadows. Engel still sang and I realized that, whatever intimate thing the king wanted to tell me, he had been right to pull me away from the raucous dance floor.

"My kingdom," he continued gently, "lies upon a green forest among hills. There are streams and waterfalls. The brooks are so close as to be heard through the window of my study while I work. As I toil, I can listen to the trickling water. The leaves perform their music in the breeze, Avva, along the beautiful winding paths among the trees in the hills. It's a beautiful and lush land. Aye, not blue, but beautiful just the same. It's my wish that one day you see my home with your own eyes."

"Our Stratos forms waterfalls running down from the Mount," I said with a nod. "And there are some waterfalls in our gardens. Ambitus Forest is thought of as the loveliest woodland in all the world. And then there's our great Mount Ambitus, so high as to reach the clouds. It is said that Olympus lies at the top, the gods surveying the entire world. And up there, everything is made of gold. So they say."

From the corner of my eye, I saw Mother rushing over; she was nearly upon us.

"So I've heard," he said, winking at me. "So I've heard. I've been to your Stratos with your mother. It is as you say. But, I've never had the misfortune of meeting lizard people." I winced. He raised a hand. "I'm so proud of you, Avivae, for what you did there. I heard of the battle from Cambria. The three of you were so brave."

I smiled and nodded. But then I searched his black eyes. "Forgive me, sir, but is there something you are trying to tell me?"

"Aye." He patted my shoulder. "So many things. You see—"

"Darius, I need you to accompany me back to our guests." It was Mother and she looked very upset. Another couple walked by us and bowed deeply before the king and queen. Mother was so angry that she completely ignored them. This time, not at me but at the king. "This is not the time, Darius. Not now."

"I can't spend time with the princess?" the king asked, squinting in irritation. "You should trust me, Delia, and not concern yourself with my words. I never forget my promises."

"Just not now, Darius," she said, raising an eyebrow. "Please. Accompany me back to our table." And she gestured for him to take her hand.

Darius nodded and feigned a smile, but I saw him squeeze his other hand tightly. For the first time, I witnessed anger from this warrior king. I could imagine that his boundless energy may not have been such a joy to his enemies on the battlefield.

"And you, Avivae," Mother said, turning to me with a fake smile. "You are neglecting your friends, my dear. Please leave us and join them, won't you?"

"Yes, Mother," I said with a bow.

"We shall talk again later, princess," Darius said with a grin and a nod.

"I'd really like that." And I really would.

7

THE GAMES BEGIN

It was another beautiful day with the bright green sun shining high above, lighting the turquoise sky. Hanna was busy, so I walked alone around fountains and statues on the ancient paths of our garden, around Amazon warrior statues, past shops and houses, then outside our gates and back into the amphitheater. I was late. Most of the seats were already taken, and there was already fighting on the field. In the center, where we had danced the previous night, four men clashed in gold hoplite armor, with the clanging of their iron swords and shields echoing all over the stadium. The crowd loved it.

Two men, kings' guards in gilded hoplite armor, ushered me up the stairs to the top level. King Darius sat at the top center, about twenty rows up. He was eating a huge drumstick, and every time he jumped up to cheer, he spit pieces of it everywhere. His joy in the sport was endearing, but his eating habits were a bit disgusting.

A few nymphs moved aside to let me through. Some hugged me as I made my way to the king. There was a space beside him reserved for one. I looked around, half expecting the general and his son would be there, but I couldn't find them. There also was no sign of Mother.

"*Anna!*" the king cried. A few more flecks of meat fell from his chin under a large grimace. "Come, come, child." Was he drunk? He certainly was flamboyant enough.

"Good morning, King Darius," I said with a bow. "Good to see you again."

"Aye, aye," he said, slapping his knee. "A wondrous day, eh?" Then he searched around him. "You want some pheasant? It's absolutely delicious. You know, the ladies of the palace suggested the bird had blue feathers. I thought they were joking, but you know, Anne, I'm in Azure so it's quite possible, isn't it?"

"Yes," I said with a smile as I sat demurely beside him. "It's probably an Azure Pheasant."

"So it is! So it is!"

I liked this king a lot. He was the most jovial man I'd ever met.

"When the horses and monokera arrive," he said, leaning over as if telling me a secret, "we shall arrange a race. It'll be glorious. I want to see how fast your unicorns are beside my warring stallions. I'd wager it'll be close. The agreement with your general was to bind their wings with ropes so that they can't fly. They shall race by foot. It will be so entertaining, don't you think?"

"But there's no question of the victor," said a very young soldier in gold armor, looking up at us from the row below.

"Yes, ours," I remarked.

He tipped his head up to me with a smile. If he hadn't been wearing the gilded hoplite armor, he wouldn't have looked much older than Marcus. The young man had a very short beard and short jet-black hair, like the king, but bright blue eyes. He was handsome.

"Uries," objected Darius, "you haven't seen them, eh? Aye, such marvelous steeds in Azurea."

"I've seen the nymph horses, sire," Uries objected. "I'm simply stating that our stallions, particularly under my care, are better at racing. You would agree if—"

Suddenly the crowd stood up and went crazy. There was only one soldier still standing on the field below, and he had a metal spear pointing down at his victim's neck.

He looked up at us.

"*Bravo! Aye, bravo!*" shouted the king, clapping. "*Another win!*"

"What will it be, king?" shouted the soldier from the field.

"Finish him!" Darius yelled heartily. That was followed by a guffaw by the king and a torrent of laughter from the crowd. It was all in jest. The whole match was merely entertainment. The soldier motioned a kill but then helped his opponent up, and the crowd cheered some more.

"Fine games, eh, Anna?" Darius asked, looking down at me. "Fine games. Are you enjoying yourself?"

I nodded and sat back down.

"As I was saying," Uries said, turning to us again, "our horses have been bred to fight. We'll show quite a sport, princess."

"Queen Harmonia once faced your men in battle, sir," I replied, "and she performed well enough defeating you."

"Aye, aye my lady," the king said with a nod. "But that be legend."

"It's not legend. It's a fact. She was my great-great-grandmother. I think you'll find Cambria has kept our monokera strong."

"If said by you, beautiful princess, I believe it," Uries said with a nod. "I look forward to witnessing it."

"We shall see soon enough, friend!" bellowed the king with more laughter.

Then he looked down at me and winked.

"Pardon me, sire," I remarked quietly to the king, "but our horses *are* the greatest in all of Gaia."

"Of course, princess," he said quietly. "Of course." He looked down at Uries and back up at me with a sly smile. "But don't you be telling Uries that, okay?"

Then I realized Darius wasn't drunk. He was just that jolly.

"Uries is a fine man," Darius continued more quietly. "You know, he's the best of my soldiers. But he's young, not much older than the general's son. A great man and, I would think, as I've been told by many ladies in Castle Cove, quite handsome. You know, he will make a great husband one day. Can you see—"

But we were interrupted again by thunderous applause.

Everyone stood up.

The horses of the Sun Kingdom, decorated in red and yellow flags over their backs, galloped into the auditorium. Violet dust swirled like a cloud behind them. The azure dust on the field was tinted purple when kicked up. Darius became so excited that he threw his pheasant leg on the ground and lifted his greasy hands, clapping wildly.

"*Bravo, bravo!*"

"I'm glad you're enjoying yourself," I said with a laugh.

"How can I not?" he cried, looking down at me. "How can you not?" Then he sat back down and leaned closer to me again. "But I was merely saying, Anne, that since you're getting older, before you know it, you'll be old enough to marry one of my men . . ." I felt my face burn with embarrassment. "You know, Uries is quite handsome. And with your little adventures, I wondered if you'd fancy him? He's very adventurous. You know, he climbs. He loves climbing hills. He jested he'd try the great Mount Ambitus itself. Get as high as Mount Olympus, he said. And, why, you're getting older and—"

"My views on boys is not your concern, sir."

It was the sharpest tone I'd given him yet. And I regretted it when I saw his face. He seemed to be struggling.

It was like he wanted to do everything he could to not hurt my feelings.

"Oh," he replied thoughtfully. "Please excuse any offense."

Then he looked back down at the field and nodded. I felt awful. But it didn't take long for him to start shouting and cheering again.

Then the soldiers were leaving the field.

I finally spotted Mother across the field. She was wearing a long glistening violet dress with a black headdress. She was near the sidelines, speaking with Cambria. Cambria was in scarlet hoplite armor. Perhaps she was preparing our soldiers for the show? It was the first time in days my mother and the king had not been together, I thought.

"What we do in battle," King Darius said to me, pointing down on the field, "is use our horses in the front lines for surprise, to overwhelm our enemy. The foot soldiers with their spears remain back and wait. This is different. Most kings, such as King Morteus and King Endrel of Caravia—" He spat away from me on the ground. "Choose spears and swords, but my family always thought this unwise. The best offense is a charge, I say, so we breed the best horses in Atala and fight with them, clearing our way through the enemy. We charge through them, Anne. Then the foot soldiers come out from behind. It had never been done before until my people in Azerban developed this technique. So effective it is that it can break the defenses of a phalanx of enemy soldiers. The phalanx is another weapon based on strict military formation. Really, only my army can mount this strategy, based on our fierce loyalty. Most of our enemies are just too unruly to mount such an offense. And anyway, we burst through any offense with our horses. The most powerful way to win is to burst through our enemy in battle, you see."

"Seems sensible, sir."

"Yes. Yes. Indeed. And it's worked to protect Azerban for many years."

"Does your kingdom have a lot of enemies?"

"Quite a few. Mainly from the Mangrin line in the South." He tore more meat with his teeth, speaking with his mouth full. "But now, the *bastar*—pardon me—that terrible and disgusting Crystal King, King Morteus—" He turned away from me and spat on the ground. "Brings in small conflicts from Shadow Forest. We do what we can, and we can do a great deal, believe me, but the enemy is cunning. I've lost many. And farther south, closer to the Strait of Aethiopia, there lie the Caravians. King Endrel is sneaky, and nasty, too, and is not on our side. And then there are the barbarians of the Hinterlands. Some in the East, close to your shores in Adelain, as well. Aye, there be many that we fight. And of the ancient, primitive, great settlement of Logenus. Old Logenth tries to remain neutral, but they fight us too. Ah, yes, my dear, there are many, many enemies in Atala. Neither your mother nor I care for any of them."

"Have they ever threatened our isle?"

Darius turned, seemingly fascinated by that question. He nodded.

"Your home, at the moment, is of particularly great concern to me," he replied. "I think you're very much like your mother. You seem more concerned with politics than lady interests, like boys."

I shook my head vehemently at that. That was certainly not true. I didn't care for politics at all; I just liked how much *he* seemed to care for it.

"We are Amazons, sir. We are interested in defense and war as much as men."

"I see."

"And you shall see it when we fight today," I said with a smile and a nod.

With that, I turned back to the games. I caught him looking at me from the corner of his eye. That made my grin wider.

Apparently Uries heard my last words. He looked up again and said, "You mean when *you* lose today, princess?"

"You'll see," I replied.

The crowds jumped up again. This time, Cambria, sitting atop Ranun, swooped down from the sky with another ten unicorns. They circled above the horses before landing before them. The entertainment was too much for Darius. He jumped up and down like a madman.

"You see!" he cried to me, pointing. "You see! Ah, such grace and strength, indeed. If I had but one of those majestic beauties in my army!"

Cambria gathered all the unicorns while men in gold armor gathered the horses. They arranged them in one line on one side of the stadium, my left side. The field beneath was very large and provided a long enough runway. Then General Cambria began tying ropes around the unicorns' torsos.

"You will lose," I said again, "even if their wings be tied." Then I added quietly, "How close is Azure Blue to being threatened?"

"Your mother hasn't told you?"

He continued to stare at the spectacle below as we spoke. Most of the unicorns were brown, but Naya and Antilus, the most royal, were a lovely white. Another two were bright red. It would take a lot of rope to bind the great feathery wings of our steeds. The unicorns hated it. But for their masters, they'd agree to it.

"Mother tells me politics doesn't concern me," I replied. "So do the Elders. They say that the Imada protects our people. But—" I turned to him. "I suppose that's precisely why it interests me. Because I don't believe them."

He nodded pensively. This was a whole other side of the king. The grease about his face was not enough to diminish the effect of his intense gaze, and I knew this was the real reason why my mother had fallen in love with him. It was not for his goofiness or bounding energy, and perhaps she hated this bravado. It was this focus, as sharp as a knife.

"Rest assured, Anne, that I shall protect your lands with my very life. I have not only fallen in love with your mother, I have fallen in love with Azure Blue. But, of course, even if I one day fail, any enemy who dares threaten you will answer to your mother's wrath."

"That's true," I said with a laugh.

"Anna, tell me," he said, patting my hand, "are you happy here in Azure?"

"Yes," I lied. "This is my home."

"I suppose it is."

Everyone jumped up again. All the horses and unicorns were lined up as the soldiers had left them and walked to the center of the field. Then Cambria and another warrior in gold beside her raised their arms in center field.

They dropped their arms.

The horses took off. I had been surprised, at first, that there was even a match. I figured our horses would swiftly defeat them. But the start looked close, and the field seemed small under the rush of the horses' hooves. I looked up at the king. He was staring with a large gaping grin. To my sides, men and nymphs were staring too. I felt bad for our unicorns. They seemed to struggle to free their bonds, but they ran hard and began to advance ahead of the horses.

Then it happened midfield. One of the unicorns, the queen's own magnificent legendary white horse Antilus, our best unicorn in the kingdom and, according to legend, Harmonia's own unicorn, tore off her bonds and flapped her great wings. Then she darted high into the air.

I screamed out her name, and she turned in the sky and seemed to look right at me, nodding, for I had ridden Antilus many times before. She was so determined to win. Then she dove down and easily crossed the finish line ahead of everyone.

All the men surrounding us booed.

"*Not fair!*" cried the king. "*Not fair!*" He looked down at me. "*Not fair at all!*"

"No, Darius. It was," I shouted, laughing. "The agreement was to bind her. No one ever said she couldn't free herself."

"Humph!" he cried and scowled at me. "Ridiculous." Then he looked down and jeered with his men.

The race ended with many of our other unicorns winning anyway. Of course they did, I had never dreamed they wouldn't, but the men had to see it with their own eyes to believe it.

Darius sat back down and folded his arms, now angry.

"Told you we'd win," I said with a giggle.

"You did."

"Not fair, my king," remarked a knight sitting beside Uries. He was an older gentleman with gray hair and massive broad shoulders. Uries chimed in with more objections too.

"Oh, well," King Darius replied, sitting down. He slapped his leg. "So be it. No rule was broken, as the princess said."

"Many of ours crossed first anyway!" claimed a nymph two rows down.

"Who am I to argue with Amazons?" asked the king, recovering his grin.

Diana, my friend Debra's mother, made her way up the aisle steps carrying a large silver dish of meat. I looked down with disgust at the king's leftover drumstick, now lying near my boot. I worried he'd get more, and I'd have to dodge more scraps by my feet. She smiled as she made her way toward the top row.

"Would you like more, sire?" Diana asked.

"Aye, aye," he said, still angry at the race. "And give the princess one, would you? It is absolutely delicious!"

"Of course." She knelt down with the tray, and I picked out a piece. "Enjoy, Princess Avivae."

"Thank you, Diana."

The king took a new piece and savagely tore it with his mouth. Then, with his mouth full, he said, "Oh how I wish I could take you to Azerban. Castle Cove is such a wondrous place. Not so incredible as here, but one that would please your eyes."

"I would love to see it."

"Ah this is so tasty! Even your food is delightful!" He laughed, looking down at his meat, seemingly forgetting the race. "You should see it, Anna. Blast all edicts! By Hades or not, you have to live, you know. You would love visiting my lands."

A couple of the nymphs nearby heard his words and started murmuring to themselves. They likely were expressing disapproval over the king's blasphemy.

As the great steeds left the field, they were replaced by archers coming from both sides of the amphitheater. Men arrived on one side and Amazon nymphs by the other. A group of twenty nymphs and a score of men came into the arena wearing pants and tight tunics, holding bows with quills tied to their backs. Their armor was not of metal, but of leather. Most of the leather armor was painted yellow. Our nymphs still wore scarlet. A few of them wore black cloths over one shoulder. These nymphs were our Imada, our most prized soldiers.

"This shall not even be a match," I quipped, folding my arms. Then I laughed at the king's expression.

"What say you now?" he asked, amused. "Princess, I like you a lot, but don't make me rethink your intelligence. My men have trained for years and are the best at the bow in all of Gaia."

"But our archers have been renowned for centuries. Since our great Queen Harmonia. Your people will not stand a chance, especially with the Imada competing."

"The ones wearing black, huh? I've heard myths of the

Imada's legendary skill. I recall it from last time. Aye, wondrous skills, indeed. This shall be delightful."

They all gathered, not unlike the way the horses had, but this time with small groups in successive rows, at the right side of the stadium. Then targets were set far down the field to my left. The men had green arrows, the nymphs red.

Arrows were fired in quick succession, with one line of archers kneeling and then being replaced by another. The Imada remained standing at the back, watching without competing. After all arrows had been fired there was an intermission, and we all waited to see the victors. It was hard to tell exactly, but I think there were far more red arrows in the center than green. Cambria and a few other Amazons in scarlet armor ran over to the targets to check them. Then they carried them over to Mother. The queen was standing ready on the sidelines. She took one arrow out of the target and lifted it high. It was a red arrow.

Nymphs everywhere jumped up and cheered.

And Darius put his head in his hand.

"I am losing my joy in this," he said.

"Wait, king," I said, pointing and chuckling. "There's more."

The nymphs wearing black over their shoulders walked forward in a line on the right side of the stadium. The Imada. All other archers exited. Then Cambria signaled to the opposite side of the amphitheater, my left, to nymphs who stood before a series of wooden cages. I wasn't sure what this was all about. The cages were glowing gold under the sunlight, as if there were yellow flames.

Cambria signaled for all the cages to be opened. A score of bright golden birds burst high into the air. These magical birds were called sun stars, the rarest birds in Azure. It was said they flew down from the golden land of Mount Olympus itself. The sight of the bright yellow birds taking flight, as bright as our green sun above, streaking through the green sky, was an amazing spectacle. For a moment, everyone just stared up with jaws dropped.

But then came the arrows. The Imada had aimed their bows up to the heavens, and they fired their blades. Each arrow was fired so quickly as to cause a yellow streak of light as birds fell to the ground. It was like the fire shows we sometimes held in the evenings, but this, with such bright birds, was at midday. This, along with the whistle of their arrows, was so beautiful. But to me, it was ghastly. When I looked at the bodies of so many birds scattered on the ground below, the loveliest birds in all of Azure Blue, I was in shock at the violence.

"*Those poor birds!*" I cried.

"Oh, come, come, princess," the King objected, furrowing his brow. "What do you think you're eating?"

"Pheasant! Not sun stars! Killing sun stars is criminal, King Darius, no matter how beautiful. This is so horrible!"

But it seemed only I was objecting. Everyone else stood staring in awe as the bright yellow streaks of light from the animals faded slowly, retaining the beauty above.

I fell back on my bench folding my arms in disgust. Then I threw my head in my hands, running my fingers through my long hair, and grunted again. All the while, the crowds still cheered.

The king touched my back. It was just him and me sitting down, I thought.

"This is what Mother does," I explained with my head in my hands. "She takes what is beautiful and destroys it. Just for sport. I've never heard of such a thing. It's all her doing. I hate her."

"That's not fair, Anne," he said, leaning close. "It's for sport. And I think every single bird was perfectly hit. There was no suffering."

"I know you care about her," I said with a shrug. "But you really shouldn't. My mother is a wicked witch, I tell you."

"She's not so bad," he said with a chuckle. "I know she loves you."

"She sure has strange ways of showing it."

I didn't know why I was telling him all this. It was one thing to discuss politics, but to talk about my mother? But as everyone stood around still stupidly cheering, it seemed intimate. I felt like I could confide in him. And I felt as if that had been what he had wanted all along.

"Why did you ask to join me today?" I asked, raising my head.

He cracked a sly smile. That got me even more suspicious. But then he dropped his drumstick again. I looked down. I was going to have to be careful where my foot landed when I left.

The crowds sat back down. I did everything I could to not look up at the sky. Those beautiful yellow streaks were still fading. And now, far worse, nymphs and men had to perform the grisly task of picking up the scores of dead glowing bodies littering the ground.

King Darius leaned toward me and quietly said, "After this half a fortnight, it will be a long time before my return, princess." Then he patted and massaged my back. "We are close to war, Anne. If war erupts, the Crystal King will try to take Castle Cove again. The bastards may even try Napea. I will have to spend every moment I have to protect our two kingdoms. That will leave little time to see you. And the secret is, Anne, I cherish this island more than my entire kingdom."

"You must do what you must do."

Below, fortunately, the sun stars had now all been collected from the field.

But I no longer thought of the birds. I thought of this king. And I felt how odd it was I should feel sad about the idea of him leaving. I had just met him.

"And there is another thing," he said. "A secret I hold that

I do not want to hold. One day, you may hate me for it, but it, too, is for the safety of our kingdom."

"What?"

"You will see . . ." He seemed about to tell me, but then he waved a finger and shook his head. "A secret, girl, is a secret."

"By the gods, now, why did I drop another leg!" he cried suddenly, looking at the ground. For a moment, I feared he'd grab the meat from the ground. "It was so delicious . . . sorry, I hope I'm not offending you, now that I know how much you care about birds."

"Sun stars," I said, rolling my eyes. I offered him my pheasant. Then I laughed when he gladly took it. "They aren't birds, King Darius. I mean, they are, but they're so special, said to be from the top of Mount Ambitus. They are said to be made of pure gold."

"Are you sure you don't want this?" the king asked, pointing at my drumstick.

"Aye."

8

MELANCHOLY AND MEN

I WENT ALONE, EARLY THE NEXT MORNING, TO OUR amphitheater. A blue fog was lifting. I could feel the moisture brush along my face. The green sun was just breaking through the mist and rising over our city walls as I turned a corner past an alleyway and headed down a winding, narrow road toward the great drawbridge. Then I made my way through the exit of our palace, across our bridge, and into the purple fields. Seeing the green rays of light burst through above, I knew it would be another lovely day in Azure Blue. Perfect for the start of our jousting tournaments.

Wish I could enjoy it. Hanna wasn't missing this time. This time she and I were hating each other. Let me tell you what had happened.

She had come alone to my bedchamber late the night before, gossiping about boys. She had spoken of Marcus and how she didn't care for him anymore. That was fine—though she needed some comforting over that too. Everything was fine, until she told me about her newest interest. Her face lit up and her eyes got all dreamy, like Mother's and the king's when they had met in the throne room a few days ago. This new boy just happened to be another boy I had mentioned that I liked. Felix. Remember? He was the tall, pale boy that had been staring at me at the dance.

I asked her why she always chose men I liked. That was the start of it.

But it wasn't the half of it. We started shouting at each other. And here it is, the absolute worst thing she could have said to me, probably the worst thing anyone had ever said to me. She blamed me for what had happened that night on the Stratos: the attack from the amphiumas. But the worst was when she blamed me for the death of my beloved Daphne. Of course, I flew into a rage. You might guess what happened next.

I supposed I could have accompanied Eva that morning. Or even Iris. But Hanna had hinted my other friends were in cahoots with her. That was the thing about my friends. See, I led them because I was their princess, but really they followed Hanna.

When I arrived at the stadium, I noticed the king sitting at the top of the steps again. He had requested to sit with me again. But the oddest thing was the person accompanying him. Engel. And Engel seemed so small beside the giant, broad-shouldered king. He was beside Engel of all people and, even weirder, I watched the two of them converse like they had known each other all their lives. I didn't even know Engel knew this king.

I climbed the stadium steps to the top.

Everyone was so excited staring down at the field. I wasn't —well, you know why. But King Darius was in as great a mood as ever, stuffing his face again with food. He wore a thin tunic and his long black hair was slicked back. His black eyes bulged looking down at the field, even when a whole lot of nothing was happening.

"My king," I said with a bow. "Greetings this morning."

"Ah, Anne!" he said, looking back, "so good to see you again, princess! Come, come, sit with me." He scooted his massive body toward Engel. "It's a beautiful morning."

"Hi, Engel."

"Hi princess," Engel said with a nod of his head. "You look lovely this morning."

Engel looked so cute. He had dressed in his best Court clothes: a long (I mean, long for him) thin robe with a tall collar and nice polished brown boots.

There was applause as lines of soldiers holding flags from Azerban walked over the blue-brown dust on the field below. They marched forward and then stood before us midfield, looking up toward the king, holding the yellow-red flags of his kingdom. And they all wore gilded hoplite armor. General Onos was in the center. And then came our army of red hoplite Amazons. The nymphs were led by General Cambria. And, as this was our home, the nymphs were met with even more applause. Cambria turned and bowed to those seated on the opposite side. She was bowing to Mother. Again, my mother sat in the center, opposite from us, on the top row. Mother was overdressed, wearing one of her most formal collared dark-violet peplos. Beside her were an entire row of white-haired nymphs in draping black peplos. We called these ladies our Elders. They were annoying hags who had never seemed particularly nice to me. Some claimed that they had personally known Harmonia. I doubted that, as Harmonia had lived centuries ago.

"I haven't seen so many soldiers in one place in a very long time," said Engel to the king, clapping. "It is good to see it in a stadium and not in battle, King Darius."

"Aye, Engel," he said, patting Engel on the back. "Aye. To peace with us, friend."

"Why is Mother not sitting beside you, Your Majesty?" I asked.

Engel leaned over the king and addressed me. "It's tradition, Avva. She sits away from the competing countries. This, and the rest of the day, represents a battle between us."

"But it is most glorious in peace," said Darius with a nod, "as you say, Engel."

"Did you two know each other before?" I asked.

"We've met a few times," replied Engel uncomfortably. "When you were little."

"Aye," the king said, turning and looking at me. "And you can have no better man to care for you than Engel."

Below it began to resemble a battleground. The nymphs stood on one side preparing their swords and spears; the men did the same on the other. The men wore their golden hoplite armor, the Amazons their scarlet.

"Avivae," Darius said excitedly, "there will be a mock battle. Two forces—why, there must be over a hundred foot soldiers down on the field! They will first square off against each other. There will be no horses. Only man versus Amazon in sword play. But today, the swords will be sharp and quite deadly."

"I know," I said. "I had asked to compete, sir."

"Did you?" He chuckled. "Of course you would."

"It was decided that she is too young," Engel remarked.

"It's ridiculous," I said. "Marcus is getting ready in the younger group, by the sidelines. And some of the others—" I pointed to a few of them donning their armor. "Sara and Gayana are just a few moons older than me, checking their shields and knives. I don't understand."

"Marcus is nearly two years older than you," Darius said. "Well, by the grace of the gods, I will return next time and I shall witness you competing in the games then."

"That will be in four years, sir," I said, even more perturbed.

"An Ambrosia, indeed, eh, Engel?" the king said, hitting

my back a little too hard. "Try to not be too upset, princess. Let us watch. Keep a good eye. The groups will dwindle to a select few, then later there will be one against one. One of my warriors against the queen's. The victor shall get a crown of olive branches to wear around his or her head. And the victor will carry an Azure rose. You know, the Azure rose is said to be immortal."

"It is immortal, sir."

He nodded.

Then he jumped like a madman, cheering again. The soldiers were arranging themselves in rows, but they stood their ground and did not yet charge.

"But all things pass eventually," I said as he sat back down.

That sounded really morose. I must have looked extremely depressed, for Engel stomped his stubby sandaled feet on the ground.

"What's the matter, Avivae?" snapped Engel. "Must I remind you that you're sitting in the presence of the king?"

"It's all right, Engel," said Darius, glancing down with a chuckle. "She can be in any mood she likes, as long as she sits beside me."

I really liked this king.

Our dancers, wearing very thin dresses, walked up the steps, offering the men and nymphs morning cakes or drinks. We all took cakes. Lots of them. Hey, I might have been in a bad mood, but that didn't mean I couldn't enjoy our delicacies. Then the king stood up, and everyone else did the same. I rose too. Men and nymphs were mixed together in groups on opposite sides of the stadium. And like in the horse race, a few Imada flying on unicorns above raised their swords. As they lowered them, the ground quaked from yet another race—this time it was people. The soldiers on the field lifted their shields and short swords and charged one another. The crash was terrible. The sound of metal clanging as swords struck shields echoed. I was worried some people would be crushed.

I looked up at the king. He didn't seem to share my worries. He was thrilled.

The games were so dangerous in a way. And this was one of the most dangerous competitions because the bodies colliding with one another made it difficult to avoid accidental death blows or fractured bones. After storming each other's shields, they jousted with their short swords. In order to claim a win, the winner had to pin down their foe or disarm them while avoiding mortally wounding anyone.

There was a great contrast between the brawn of the king's soldiers and the agility and dancelike movements of my sister nymphs. Some worked together in teams. But ultimately, that strategy would be short-lived. There could only be one adult and one young adult victor this Olympiad. I saw Cambria. Her style was a work of art. Her grace flowed around the bodies of men. She pinned one down with the tip of a blade and then rolled over another with her shield. She seemed faster than any warrior too. Then I spotted the massive General Onos. Fortunately, he was nowhere near my instructor at the moment. He was gathering nymphs by the bundle and striking them down. And all the while, from above, the chaos was surveyed by a group of Amazons atop our monokera. This was our Imada. They did not fight—instead they claimed losers by throwing down red flags over their stunned bodies. Per custom, if a flag hit you, you had to leave the field. Anyone who cheated was picked up by the Imada themselves.

Then I saw something that made my skin burn. Hanna! Of all ignoramuses, incompetent and stupid nymphs, my former best friend—who I really hated at that moment—wore scarlet armor with a shiny new helm, preparing on the sidelines to compete.

I shrieked.

Engel turned. My body shook in rage. How could my

mother stop me from joining the games but let her fight! Hanna and I were only a couple moons apart in age!

I shrieked again.

"What is it now, Avva?" asked Engel, crouching near the king's stomach to talk to me.

I just pointed at the sidelines in disgust. The king was looking down at me, amused. It wasn't for long. He quickly looked back at the fight.

"Why is Hanna down there!" I cried.

Engel leaned behind the king to talk to me. Meanwhile the king kept jumping up and down.

"Your friend is older than you."

"How, Engel? Hmm? Four moons? Four moons!"

"She's older," Engel said, barely loud enough to be heard. He was trying not to disturb the king. But Darius looked like nothing could distract him.

"Engel, she can barely hold a sword!" I cried. "How can Cambria allow her to fight but not me! All I asked this morning was to be a part of today's battle. I didn't even ask for solo combat."

"Did you see that!" cried the king. "By the gods, did you see that!"

"She doesn't want you to fight, Blue," Engel said.

"The queen or Cambria?"

"Are you two all right?" asked the king, furrowing his brow.

"It's nothing," Engel said. "Please just enjoy the games, sire."

"Aye," King Darius said with a guffaw. "Who cannot? Aye. Aye, *aye*! And look, friend! Only a few are left standing!"

But the battle was over. The Imada rounded up all the losers and led them off the field. Knives and swords were strewn around on the blue ground, their metal reflecting emerald under the green sun above. A few shields, red and gold, had been left too. And many wounded were now being tended along the sidelines by Amazon healers. There had been no fatalities. Thank the gods. From what I'd heard, four years ago, there had been two deaths during the initial battle.

"You all right, Anne?" King Darius asked, sitting down.

I shook my head.

"What's the matter?"

Then he started eating a powdered cake. I wasn't sure where he had gotten it. He was eating it disgustingly, getting white powder all over his black beard.

"Never mind her," Engel said, scowling at me. "She gets like this from time to time." Then he reached behind the king, tapping my shoulder. "Iris isn't preparing. Neither is Maili or Kendra. You need to stop acting like a spoiled brat."

"She's a princess," the king said with a shrug. "If she wants to be spoiled, let her."

"I don't know what's gotten into her, Darius," Engel said. "I really don't. She's in such a mood this morning. Sorry."

"Being with her is all that I can ask for," Darius said. "I don't care. Even if she cries." Then he looked down at me with a tender smile. "That is, I don't care if you *choose* to cry, my dear girl. Just your company brings me joy enough."

"You're always too kind to me, sir," I said, blushing. And he was. "Cambria has taught me well. I could fight the next battle. I'm ready. I'm the best in my class at swordplay."

"I don't doubt it."

I heard the banging of drums. Then the audience added to the bass by stomping their feet on the wooden planks of the steps. The whole auditorium seemed to shake. Cambria, General Onos, and only a handful of other victors were the only ones left on the field. They all bowed together to the crowds, and that was met by a torrent of applause. They were victorious and would compete with only a handful of others after our break. Then three groups of ten Amazon dancers took to the field below with long, beautifully woven multicolored streamers. They wore tight brown leather tunics and pants, as was our custom, the same casual clothes I wore today. They ran at great speeds, flipping and twirling with the streamers waving around them.

As they danced, I looked across and watched Mother speaking to one of the old ladies beside her. That made me wonder. *Mother isn't allowed to sit with the king during the games? Was that an excuse? Is she fighting with this king?* No. Mother glanced across the field at us. She wasn't looking at me; she was staring at the king. She seemed so stricken by him.

When the green sun rose directly above us, we all went down the stairs of the amphitheater into the huge nearby tents for an afternoon meal. I said goodbye to the king but promised I'd return later for the final match. Then I nodded and greeted many of my mother's friends and heard them talk of how wonderful the show had been that morning. There was gossip of those injured, but thankfully I heard it was only a handful. The worst was Vincius, a young adult male, who apparently had been cut savagely across his left arm. Many of the men feared his injury might be permanent. But, otherwise, most had come out of the ordeal with only cuts and bruises. Then they spoke of the victors, our great generals, of course.

The huge tents were lit inside by torches. I passed Hanna. She excitedly waved. Leave it to Hanna for it to take only one morning to forget the worst fight of our lives. I ignored her. I was still mad.

Then I walked alone to the only empty wooden table left at the very end of the Hall. For me to do this—a princess no less—caught every wandering eye in the Hall, especially those of my friends. Not to mention, Mother had asked me to wear one of my formal royal dresses, and I had chosen a tunic and pants. I spotted Mother across the Hall; she was giving me disapproving glances.

Diana approached my empty table. She offered me dates, olives, and cheeses on a silver platter.

"Princess, what are you doing here? Debra's over there with your friends."

"Resting," I said with a sigh. Resting from what? Who knew.

Diana shrugged her shoulders and poured me a glass of myrle berry juice from a pitcher. Then she laid a bunch of cheeses and dates on my plate.

"Is everything all right?" Diana asked quite amicably before leaving. She had a tender smile. Kind Diana, she was as kind as her daughter Debra. I loved Debra like a sister.

"Never mind. I'm fine."

"Try to enjoy the rest of the games, princess. They only come once every four years, you know."

And that only made me feel worse.

Then I looked across the tent at my friends. Iris and Kaila were looking over, amused at something. I lost my smile.

"Is this table open?"

I lurched back. Standing over me was a blemish-ridden face with long bright blond hair and skin as white as snow. Felix. Remember? The boy that stupid Hanna wanted now that Marcus had rejected her—because *I* wanted him. Well, he hadn't gone over to Hanna's table, had he?

"I'm Felix."

"Uh," I said with a shrug. "Yeah. I mean . . . why not? No. Sure. I mean, no . . . I mean, that is to say, no, nobody's here. Go right ahead. I'm the princess."

Stupid. He probably knew I was the princess.

"How are you liking the games, Princess Avivae?" he asked very formally with a sweet smile. Then he plopped down across from me. Like me, he leaned on his side, as was the tradition of the Hinterland men.

I leaned over the table, cupping my mouth as if telling him a secret. "I'd have liked them a lot more if I could compete. Mother is forbidding me."

"How dare she." Then he smiled again. And then,

wouldn't you know it, I caught Iris snickering with my friends. Hanna wasn't. Hanna was staring with her mouth open like a fish.

"She's probably punishing you for what happened to Daphne," Felix said.

"*Not you too!*" I snapped. Poor Felix looked devastated by my explosion. "Do you think Daphne's death is my fault?"

"No. No," he said, raising a hand, "of course not. Princess—"

"Call me Avva," I said gruffly, brushing my long hair back and leaning back on my side. "I . . . I just loved Daphne so much. That's all. And I really miss her."

"I didn't mean to get you upset. I only meant that your mother was probably punishing you for all that happened, that's all. It was a terrible storm. And I heard that your life was in danger." He looked down at my plate. I hadn't touched it. "Hey, you gonna eat those dates?"

I shook my head and pushed the plate toward him. He gladly gobbled some up.

Then I looked over at my friends again. Now that Felix was here, they were having the time of their lives. Only Hanna wasn't joining in their laughter.

"Will you be competing tonight in the main battle, Felix?" I asked, trying to ignore them.

"Well, Marcus clipped me in practice." He showed me bandages on his right arm. "I didn't even see him coming. It was a cheap trick. He seemed to be injuring everyone he didn't want to fight in the tournament. He's a cheater."

"I'm not surprised."

"Yeah, well, I'll try to compete later. You know we all take so much pride in your games. We look forward to it." Then he snatched another date from my plate. With his mouth full, he said, "I'm pretty sure he was cheating."

"Marcus is a pompous idiot."

"Huh, I thought you two were close?" Felix asked

pensively. "You went together in the storm, didn't you? Well, I'll still fight. Hey, aren't you gonna eat anything?"

"Not really hungry."

He had such light blue eyes. His hair was wavy. He was cute, facial blemishes and all. Come to think of it, I didn't think he was any less attractive than Marcus, maybe more so. He reached for my plate and touched some sliced cheese. "You want this?"

"Did you come to my table to eat my lunch?"

"Sorry, Avivae," he said, pulling back. His face flushed red. Poor boy. His skin was so white that it didn't take much to embarrass him. But that was cute too.

"Go ahead." I said, laughing again. "Take it. I'm really not that hungry."

He pulled the plate closer to him, which made me giggle. Then he looked over at me with a smile.

Iris was whispering in Debra's ear just to get me mad. I knew she couldn't care less what she said—she just wanted me to *see* that she was talking about us. Iris was Queen Gossip. Had I not been speaking with Hanna's crush, Hanna would probably have joined her.

"Can I ask you something, Felix?"

"Sure," he said with his mouth full.

"Are you and Andalay together?"

"Andalay?" he asked, surprised. "What makes you think that?"

"Is she, or . . . was she your girlfriend? I heard in the Court the story about you two. How you got stranded at sea and landed on the shores of Napea during a rainstorm. And that she and her family cared for you when you were ill a few years ago. But I haven't seen her near you on the field or at the dance. I thought you two were close."

"Who told you we were together?"

"Just wondering."

"Andalay is really nice. I remember spending time with

her when we were kids. I think she was eight and I was nine. Yeah, we were together at her house when her mother tended to me. That was before the last festival." He shrugged and looked off for a moment in thought. He had strong cheekbones and fierce hawk-like eyes. "You were probably six." He laughed. I didn't think that was funny. "So when I came over by ship this time, yeah, I was looking forward to seeing her. So, I talked with her." Then he just shrugged his shoulders and coughed. He drank a glass of dark red juice—my myrle berry juice. I loved that. "She's a nice girl."

Just a nice girl?

"Oh . . . I'm sorry, is this your juice?" he asked, holding up my wooden cup.

"Not anymore," I said. Then his look of concern made me burst into laughter. I didn't laugh long. It was echoed by my former friends. Felix noticed them for the first time. *Oooh*, I wanted to kill them.

"What gave you the idea that we were *together*?" he asked.

"Just heard something like that."

He furrowed his eyebrows but then stiffened, sat up straighter, and acted all formal. "My greatest honor in the games shall be having the company of the princess of Azure. When I saw the princess by her lonesome, I thought she needed some company."

"My friends aren't smart," I said with a laugh. "They know just how to hurt someone, you know?"

"I can't see how anybody would ever want to hurt you."

And then he did it. He stared into my eyes. And I just got lost in his. I think we just looked into each other's eyes for the longest time—it probably would have been all night if it hadn't been for more snickering from my wicked so-called friends.

"That's nice, Felix," I said, finally averting my gaze. "Very nice. Thank you."

He grabbed the wooden cup of juice again, my myrtle juice, revealing his anxiety with his shaking hand.

"I think Andalay is an idiot," I said.

I regretted that right after I said it. It seemed all I was doing was saying bad things about everybody to the nicest boy I'd ever met. He even furrowed his brow again, not seeming to approve.

"Why?"

"She's, well, not very nice to my friend Hanna. She's . . . what's the word? Uppity. You know the word, Felix? Like Marcus. It means conceited. Arrogant."

"I know the word, but I'm not sure I agree. Andalay's always been nice to me and my family."

"It's just, she's always been mean to Hanna. Not to me . . . of course, 'cause I'm the princess. But to Hanna. And . . . Debra. She picks on people who are younger than she is."

Why did I say that!? I just reminded him how much younger I am! I began to feel a strong urge to crawl in a hole.

So, what was I to do? Suddenly act nice? That could seem fake.

Well, that would be better than insulting everyone we knew, I suppose.

"Which is your father?" I blurted. I think I just wanted to say anything. "I didn't see you with any of the men."

"My mother brought me here." That was odd. Few men took their wives to the games.

"Mother had to," he explained. "Father passed away a couple years ago on a campaign protecting King Darius's chief adviser, Henri Untair. Henri is our court wizard and adviser. Henri is a very close personal friend to the king. Well, my father, one of General Onos's most favored soldiers, was told by Onos to scout alone and keep surveillance over the wizard's home. This was a great honor for my father. Alone, Father watched the Crystal King's spies who had ambitions of taking Henri's home in Shadow Forest. From what I heard,

Onos had a terrible fight defending the wizard's home. My father was ambushed and killed on the same day that Henri was captured."

He stopped and looked away. It seemed telling me all this pained him. So I took his hand. He stared at my hand for a moment and smiled again. Then he nodded.

"It happened a long time ago, Avva."

"You don't have to tell me."

"You have such beautiful blue eyes, princess," he said with a nod, gazing back at me.

I let go of his hand and shrugged. "All nymphs have blue eyes."

"Yes, but yours are the prettiest I've seen." Then his face turned a brighter red than ever. "My . . . father died honorably, Avivae. General Onos was devastated. He and the general were very good friends."

My friends stopped laughing. Perhaps they sensed how intimate we had become.

"It's said he took down five or six Crystal warriors before he was slain in the forest," he said. "Father was an amazing swordsman. It was the boy, Sol, who scouted the area alone and reported seeing my father's body. I suppose . . ." He stopped for a moment, his blushing almost gone. "I was told General Onos rescued Henri and the boy shortly afterward. I suppose, so many things in life have to do with timing. Wouldn't you say, Avva?"

"I'm so sorry, Felix."

"So, my mother took me here alone. That is the reason for the handful of other mothers here at the games. If we go to war, and we surely will, I'm afraid, there will be quite a few more boys coming with their mothers to the next Olympiad. My mother knows that my father would have wanted me to compete. But she is one of the few ladies of King Darius's court to travel with us. She and I are staying in Andalay's home, instead of the men's barracks. Maybe that's where all this gossip regarding Andalay is coming from."

"Could be."

"Guess I am with her, in a way." He chuckled and, again, looked deeply into my eyes. "Seems your friends aren't so dumb?"

I laughed and ran my hand through my long hair. I would have laughed more—for I felt happier than I had in a very long time—had it not been for an eruption of laughter bellowing from my stupid friends. They were at it again.

We heard bells clang, and everyone got up excitedly for the recommencement of the afternoon games. I didn't. I still wanted to talk to my new friend.

"Avva," he said, looking down.

"Yes."

"Do you think we could meet again tonight after the games?"

"Sure. Where?"

"Uh . . ."

"Do you know the maze?" I asked. "The garden maze in the palace?"

"Of course, it's amazing. I was shown it when we first arrived. Bushes are green in our lands. Yours are blue."

"Why don't you meet me there right after the banquet, Felix. We can meet on one of the benches by the entrance."

"All right. I look forward to it, princess. Tonight then."

I looked into those innocent blue eyes. Then I glanced at the blemishes along his forehead. If only those blemishes weren't there. It was the only thing wrong with him, really. So? Who cared? He seemed so nice and brave. And cute.

I really liked him. Yes, I liked him a lot.

He bowed chivalrously before me and then caught up with some of the other men.

I got up and headed to the exit. But that meant I had to pass by my friends' table.

They all turned their backs on me, pretending to ignore me. Apparently, now *they* were mad at *me*.

"*I'll meet you tonight, lover,*" repeated Iris, cackling like an idiot.

Ooohh, she was gonna get it. I marked it down in my mind. After she apologized, and it wouldn't be long, I would make sure that, one way or another, all these girls would get it.

"See you at the games, Avva," Hanna said, looking back at me. She was the only one who seemed serious. "And I don't hate you anymore."

9

THE GAMES WE PLAY

I WALKED BACK TO THE AMPHITHEATER FEELING ON TOP OF THE clouds. I was to be with a man that night, the sweetest, nicest boy I'd ever met! What a difference compared to how I was feeling before. I felt like I was flying. I was already planning our evening. I'd show him the maze, maybe lead him astray and get him lost for fun. Then I'd show him our zoo. We have such wonderful creatures there that he's probably never seen. Then maybe I'd tour him around Crystal Palace, among the statues, gardens, and waterfalls. It would be such a wonderful night, just like it had been a perfect day. It wasn't too cold or too hot. My daydreaming was interrupted when I almost tripped in the aisle walking back up to the king's seat. Fortunately, Engel was just returning to the aisle and grabbed me by the arm before I fell.

"Thanks, Engel."

"Be careful, princess."

I nodded.

"You still mad?" Engel asked.

"What would I be mad about?"

He looked at me suspiciously. Engel had raised me ever since I was a baby. He knew better than anyone about my ways and probably could, by now, read my mind. His curious expression made me laugh. Perhaps later, I'd tell him what had happened. No, I was sure I would. I told that dwarf everything.

"Anna!" cried Darius, slapping his leg and getting up. He kept addressing me by the Atalan pronunciation of my name. I loved that. "Princess Anne, I've had so much fun that now I feel a bit sad, like you. The tournaments will soon be over. But —" He looked me over curiously. "You don't seem as sad as before, my dear."

"I feel fine, sir."

"I see," he said, gathering me up and hugging me a little too long, embarrassing me before all the other spectators. "It's so good to see you. I can already smell food. Can you? I hear tonight will be the best of all feasts. Your people have foods that are as glorious as your lands."

"I don't think I can eat much more."

"You're so thin," remarked the king. "You should enjoy all of it."

"I'll try," I said with a laugh.

Well, before I couldn't eat because I was in a lousy mood. Now, I didn't want to eat because I was up in the clouds. Then again . . . I could do with a little food. I was hungry. Come to think of it, I hadn't eaten breakfast, and I had given all my lunch to Felix.

As if on cue, Diana climbed the steps to the top row with more treats: lemon nut cakes and olive bread. This time I reached for her tray and grabbed a handful of cakes. I remembered preparing them earlier with Diana in the kitchens. So, why not? The king grabbed one and then simply smiled, looking down at me. Past the king's broad shoulders, I caught Engel giving me a disapproving look for grabbing too many. That was Engel's forte, always showing disapproval. Him and Mother.

A group of men clad in gold and women in scarlet,

wearing iron and leather hoplite armor, walked slowly toward the center of the field. Each soldier carried a shield in one hand and a short sword in the other, though a few carried nets. I guessed, unlike the great battle in the morning, there were maybe only twenty on each side.

I saw Onos and Cambria walking and laughing together. It was a pity, I would much rather have seen them angry at each other in preparation for the upcoming fight.

I looked at the king and he winked at me.

"The victor, of course, shall be a nymph," I said.

"We'll see, princess. We'll see. The evening is young."

"The children will be out after the men today, King Darius," Engel added.

Each soldier tested their blade, checking its sharpness, then moved on to readjusting their shin and elbow guards or readjusting their helmets. Onos and Cambria were still having a great old time socializing. They seemed to be the only ones not nervous. Then a nymph dressed in a long black dress—a white-haired old woman named Milda, one of the leaders of our Elders and Imada, came out onto the field and drew a long sword. She stood between the two groups. I couldn't completely discern Milda's face from that distance, but I could hear the sudden clang of the soldiers' metal boots and armor as they all fell simultaneously into their fighting stances at the rise of her sword. The audience stood quiet and still. I caught my mother standing at the opposite end of the stadium again. I wondered if it would be a victory for her or the king. Milda swung her sword down, and the groups charged each other again. The sudden clash echoed around the stadium. This battle was not a stampede, but deadlier by sword and shield and with greater skill. Many in the audience seemed nervous, even the king.

My eyes fell on Onos and Cambria. Their skills were rivaled by no one, and they quickly subdued any attacker. At one point, they "cheated" a little, standing back to back fending off attackers. One parried while the other thrusted, and every time either one of them held a blade to the enemy's throat, the Imada quickly intervened on a flying unicorn with the tip of a spear and pushed the loser off the field.

Then, quite suddenly, there were gasps. I didn't understand until I turned away from my favorite champions. One of the contenders, her name was Ruby, had fallen with a sword stuck savagely into her thigh. Her opponent, one of the men on the general's teams, yanked off his helm and fell over her in concern. Many Amazons swooped down from the air upon unicorns, stopping the battle. The crowd grew silent as soldiers crouched around her.

Then they cheered as Ruby rose and was helped by Imada and her opponent over to the sidelines.

"Oh, by the gods, I hope she's all right," said Engel, shaking his head. "That wound seemed deep."

"Aye," said the king. "Aye. But it wasn't a mortal wound, friend." He turned to me and nearly had to shout among all the cheers from the crowd. "Do you know her, Anne?"

"Ruby," I replied, staring down and nodding. "She's a member of the Imada and a very good friend of the leader of the Elders, Milda. She's one of our best swordswomen. Also, the best dancer in Court."

"I could see it. She swung the blade quicker than Henri. But that's a nasty wound. Not sure she'll be dancing for a while, I'm afraid."

More Imada came to the sidelines to help Ruby, but the fight continued.

"It's not fair, really," continued Darius. "This Ruby of yours would have lasted much longer, I think. Such a wondrous fighter."

"But she was cut, sir."

"Aye. But did you see how? She was distracted and pushed by the man behind her."

"So it is in battle."

"Aye," he said with an admiring smile. "So it is in life, Anna."

I shrugged. "It seems—"

I couldn't finish my sentence. The crowd cried out again. This time it was another fallen, but it looked far worse. Cambria apparently had placed her sword on the neck of an adversary to mark a win, and it had been pushed deeper into his neck when she was hit from behind by another foe. If the blade had sunk into his neck—which I still was unsure of—the man was surely dead.

"*Who has fallen!*" cried Engel. "*By the gods, another!*"

The king just shook his head, staring.

This strike was brutal enough for the Imada to stop the fight. Cambria was so shaken that another adversary was able to throw a net on top of her. She ignored the net completely. Then another Imada from the air swooped down and stopped that same man from charging her with his sword.

Onos slid to his knees on the dirt beside the fallen man. The man wasn't moving.

Everyone remained standing still.

"Is that Thasius, my lord?" asked Engel.

All joy left King Darius as he stared. But he said nothing.

The soldiers cleared. Only a handful of soldiers, Onos and Cambria, and the Imada who had dismounted from their unicorns, stood over the fallen man.

I looked across the field and saw my mother rush down the steps. All her subjects opened a path. She moved so swiftly that her long violet dress fluttered behind her. Then she crouched over the fallen body. She remained over him for the longest time, but I still couldn't make out whether the man was dead or just gravely injured. All I could see under my mother was a motionless body.

She cocked her head up and shouted, "*Engel! Engel!*"

"Engel, by the gods, go down and help quick!" cried the

king. "Go down now, man, and see if there's anything you can do to heal him."

"Yes, sire."

He hobbled as fast as the queen had, down our steps and across the field. Once again, everyone moved to allow him passage.

"I think he's dead," I said.

There was really no point in saying that, and I hated myself for it. The king, rightfully, didn't respond. Of course, Cambria wouldn't be blamed. Everyone who played the games knew the risks. But death, the worst outcome, was never welcomed by anyone. I knew Cambria—I knew her better than anybody. I knew she'd be devastated over this kill.

Engel crouched over the fallen man, lifting his limp arm, checking his neck. Then he walked over to Cambria and hugged her by the waist. That sent Cambria falling to her knees crying. Her crying was contagious amid the crowds. We all knew what it meant.

Then Engel slowly, with his head heavy, approached the center field. He shouted, "He's dead, King Darius."

The crowd became unruly. I heard some actually accuse Cambria of murder. That enraged the king.

"*You all knew the risks!*" King Darius cried, gnashing his teeth. I could not believe how loudly his voice bellowed. "No one is to blame! Anyone foolish enough to accuse her answers to me and the queen!"

The objections quieted. But now the king was beside himself in anger. He seemed to have to force himself to sit down.

"Thasius is old," the king finally said quietly to me. "He fought with me in the Crystal Kingdom at the time of my father. He was . . . one of my best guards. He's very dear, princess. Almost . . . like a father, I suppose. And I think he means the same to the army."

"I'm so sorry."

"Aye." He forced a smile. "Aye. But . . . but, he wouldn't have been ashamed of dying in this wondrous land of yours. No, he . . . he wouldn't. He would consider his fall an honor."

I placed a hand on his shoulder. He looked at me curiously. Then he lost his scowl.

But then, it seemed the melancholy was too much for him.

"*Continue the games!*" he cried, leaping up. "*That is what Thasius agreed to, and it is what he would have wanted!*"

They looked at my mother, who still knelt over the body. Her face seemed so grave. But she rose and simply nodded. Cambria was still crouched down, refusing to exit the field.

Engel slowly made his way back up our steps.

"It is the way, friend," the king said as Engel sat back down.

It seemed to be the wrong thing to say. It made Engel look furious.

"Savage," Engel said in disgust, spitting on the ground. "It's hard enough that your subjects must die in war, but to have to pass in—"

"Engel," said the king, raising a finger. "Enough. I know your opinions. Enough of this. This *is* preparation for war."

"I'm not sure Cambria will have it in her to continue," I said.

"She will, Anne," said Darius. "She must. She will go on for the man's honor. Otherwise his death shall have no meaning."

"No, Darius," I objected, staring at her. She still kneeled, with her head down, in center field. "Cambria has the greatest heart of all our people."

"Doesn't matter," he said, shaking his head. "She'll fight. It is what Thasius would have desired, I say. Just you wait and see."

I wasn't so sure.

I looked at Engel. He seemed to be struggling with a great

deal on his mind, but he didn't say a word. He just kept rubbing his stubby hands together nervously.

After more silence, my little friend spoke again. I knew he shouldn't have.

"Now we wait for the next to fall," he said.

Darius stared at Engel. "*I said, enough!*" he yelled. His fury reminded me of my wicked mother.

"You should call off the rest of the games," Engel said, looking down.

I was in disbelief that Engel wouldn't obey the king. Engel's such a strange fellow, you know, always bowing and respectfully responding to authority, but never fearing to speak his mind. When this dwarf had something to say, he just said it. He didn't care about the consequences. And I didn't fully understand his objections. I heard four people died last Olympiad.

"Calling off the games would disgrace him," I reminded Engel, more to calm down the king.

"Aye," said the king morosely with a nod. "Aye, the princess is right."

"It won't," Engel said. "And you need to stay out of this, Avva."

Then Engel dared to meet the king's gaze.

"You will stop talking about this, dwarf," said Darius, wagging a finger. "I warn you, you will stop or I will carry you down to the field myself and give you the same fate as Thasius."

"No, you'll give it to another one of your subjects."

I couldn't believe Engel had said that. And I was not sure Darius could either. I wondered if Darius had ever heard such disrespect before. But I had heard Engel act disrespectfully like this, many times before, to my mother.

The king jumped up and shouted, "*Get out! Get out of my sight, you purple demon!*"

"I'll join the queen," Engel said with a deep bow. "Perhaps she will put a stop to it."

"*You go do that, you infernal wretch!*" Darius said, seething. "The queen will not stop the games over a single fallen man, you idiot!"

"Your Majesty, people are staring," I said. He whirled around with wild eyes. But then he seemed to calm at the sight of me.

He nodded gruffly, folding his arms in a huff, falling back down in his seat.

I watched Engel hobble down the steps and to the other side of the amphitheater. He walked up the steps where stood the queen. But when he reached my mother's seat, it seemed like Mother started quarreling with him too.

Finally, Cambria stood up in the field. Imada accompanied her. And the crowd responded with thunderous applause. I pointed and grabbed the king's arm, mainly to try to get him out of his rage over Engel. Darius rose and clapped.

"You see," he said. "You see, aye, I told you. This is your greatest Amazon warrior. She cannot *not* fight."

The rest of the show was uneventful. It seemed the death cast a shadow on the remaining fighters when they returned. No one wanted to make the same fatal mistake again. Even so, injuries were still unavoidable. Even in mourning, Cambria still managed to stave off fighters. As did General Onos.

When the two were the last standing, they bowed before King Darius, and then my mother. They would fight in solo combat now.

"Well, I could have predicted this," remarked the king.

"But Cambria won't win tonight against Onos," I said. "She's too disturbed by today's events."

"Really, Anne? I don't believe it. This is the first time you're predicting a victory for me."

"I told you, I know Cambria's heart. She's too good."

"Pity. I'm sure my general won't let her win over it."

The field cleared. Then everyone waited for the final battle.

Cambria and Onos stood center field, facing each other. Cambria in her best scarlet armor, Onos in gold. They both took a fighting stance, crouched low before each other. Two Imada soldiers atop monokera swooped down, raising their swords.

They lowered their swords.

Cambria circled around Onos, twirling her short sword from side to side in her right hand while carrying the shield in the other. I could already imagine the words of my trainer running through her own mind: *"Keep a good footing for balance, shield your body with your blade so that there is no opening, strike without thought, use fear to simply move you, watch your enemy and learn from her mistakes . . ."* No doubt, she was ruminating on all this now.

They clashed. With great speed, Cambria dodged a blow to her head while hacking at an opening near Onos's right thigh. Onos parried, contorting his body more than I had imagined possible for such a large man, and then swung back, hurling Cambria down to the ground.

Cambria rolled.

"What skill!" cried the king, for the first time forgetting his grief. *"By the gods, such a sight to see!"*

Cambria leaped up and charged him, swinging her blade and coming in contact with his shield. The metal clang rang through the stadium, and deafening cheers fell from the crowd. I thought that the charge would cause Onos to tumble on the ground. It didn't. He fell to his knees, but then he jumped back to his feet and swung at her helm. She swung her sword from behind her head and caught his sword with her blade. Then, spinning around, she fought blade to blade, parry to parry, across the field. The king was loving it, jumping up and down like a little boy. There seemed no end to the strike and counter parry, until finally Cambria managed to trip the giant man onto his back. She leaped over him and pointed her sword at his neck. But then . . . she hesitated. *Because of Thasius?* This might have cost her the match. Onos used her delay to swipe his shield hard against her body, throwing her to the ground. Then he wrestled her, turned her on her back, and finally put his own sword to her throat.

A red flag fell onto Cambria. Onos had won.

So many nymphs everywhere booed while the men were jumping up and down like crazy. The king's enthusiasm, which usually amused me, annoyed me this time.

"*Aye! Of course, Onos won!*" he shouted looking down to me. "*Of course!*"

But I knew Cambria had only lost because of Thasius.

General Onos helped Cambria up and then turned to us and bowed. General Onos received even greater applause. And then Onos, the victor of the games, looked along all the stadium seats. He shouted at the crowd, asking if anyone challenged him. This was according to custom. All final victors could still be challenged. Few ever dared. It was a disgraceful act toward the victor, and rage over such an audacious dispute could, and had, it was said, led to death.

No one challenged him. And so Mother rushed down the steps and moved gracefully across the field, carrying an olive branch twisted into a crown. She kissed Onos's cheek and laid the olive branch crown over his head. Cambria bowed to him. The match was over.

10

BY MY RIGHT

After an intermission, while our nymphs danced on the field, it was the *children's* turn, as Engel had called us. This made me angry again. Not Engel's belittling remark. I mean, some said he was a thousand years old. But *the children's turn* meant that, had Mother allowed it, it would have been *my* turn.

A group of young men and nymphs crowded the field. I spotted Hanna of all people. And then I saw Felix. And Marcus too. Marcus walked arrogantly with his head up, now likely bolstered by the victory of his father.

"Which of your friends do you hope will win, Avva?" asked the king.

"Who cares."

"What do you mean?" he asked, amused.

"Remember, King Darius, I won't be there, so I don't see how it matters."

"Still upset, huh? Well, at least you're not like Engel. You're not thinking of peaceful dreams like that fool."

"I love Engel more than anything."

"Aye, aye, I do too," he said with a sigh. "Who doesn't love Engel? But he seems to get in a fight with me every time I visit. He hates this competition just as much as he hates battle. But like I told him, it's this competition that prepares us. But you, you seem quite the opposite. You are a true Ambrosia, angry for not competing, eh?"

"I told you before, sir, I was trained by General Cambria. I can probably beat any one of your subjects down on the field."

"I don't doubt it," he said with a sparkle in his eye. "Delia's daughter, indeed. Well, if it were up to me, and not your mother, you would compete. But . . . you don't want any of your friends down there to win?"

"None of them are my friends."

"I see."

My eyes fell on Marcus. When the Imada lifted their swords, it was Marcus who I watched. As much as his overconfidence irritated me, I knew he was the best fighter. I wondered if he would kill someone accidentally like Cambria had. It usually was the most skilled warriors who did terrible things like that. I'd found that it was the heroes, like Cambria, so driven to win that they didn't have it in their makeup to do otherwise.

As they all began clashing swords and shields, no one died. Rather, Marcus and another boy named Polius rapidly became the last standing in the field. Felix was called out. Of course, Hanna was taken out at the first strike—no surprise there. No Amazon nymphs were victorious. Because I hadn't been allowed to compete.

Polius was Uries's younger brother, so Uries, who had remained remarkably quiet a couple rows down, went crazy when he saw who was challenging the general's son.

Polius was a rather stocky, muscular teenager, much bigger than the more fit Marcus. The two faced off against one another in center field, and when the Imada lowered their swords, they charged. It was vicious. It was brawn against skill, and I could tell who would be the victor even before he won.

There never was any hope for Polius. A few times, because he was so massive, he managed to grab Marcus and hurl his body a few paces along the blue-brown dust, but Marcus quickly leaped up like a spider and crashed his sword against the giant boy's shield.

Finally, with just the right angle, Marcus managed to turn his blade against the boy's neck.

Uries cried out in anger.

"Now that was a good fight, Uries," countered the king. "Very fair. Well done. Good fight! Bravo!"

I disagreed but said nothing. It had all been over too fast.

My mother walked down the steps across from us, with smiles, holding another olive crown. And that was it. The games were over. Everything was done, and all the men would go home.

Marcus went through the formality of shouting out the traditional challenge to the audience regarding any remaining challengers.

But that's when everything changed. To the crowd's shock, someone shouted out *"Aye!"* My mother halted halfway down the field.

"Interesting," said the king, running his fingers through his beard pensively. He slowly sat back down. As the challenger made his way through the sidelines, I recognized him. Felix.

Felix!? What in Hades are you doing, you idiot? Marcus is going to kill you for threatening his prize!

"That fool!" I snapped. "Any challenger will be violently fought. He could lose his life!"

"It's his choice, Anna. Very brave. Felix is bound to be one of my greatest soldiers one day. And if he falls now, he, like great Thasius, shall die in honor in your lands."

"But I don't want anything to happen to him."

"You like this boy?" Darius asked curiously.

"Yes. I like him. He's very nice."

"Engel is very nice. This challenger best be better than nice to beat Onos's son."

"I saw Marcus fight the amphiuma. He's not so great."

Darius laughed over that.

The sun was beginning to sink under the great Mount Ambitus as we waited for the Imada to start the challengers' fight. In center field Felix was putting on his wrist bands while Marcus was twirling his short sword. Marcus looked incensed with rage. And then, as the sun fell further, a blue shadow fell across the fields darkening everything. Torches were lit all around the stadium.

The Imada had the two boys face each other. Then Felix looked right up at me. *Me*. Right up at me. And he bowed. I think the king believed he was bowing for him, but I knew the truth. I was absolutely sure he was bowing to me.

Are you risking your life for me, stupid boy!

"Are you all right, Anna?" Darius asked. No, my heart was raging. I felt faint. I turned and the king was staring at me. "You seem concerned."

"I'm fine. Just fine."

"Hmm. You seem very worried. You were in such a better mood earlier." Then he angered me, as he had the day before. "I haven't seen you so interested in the games since your general lost. And I think that I saw you sitting alone with this boy during the break. Do you fancy him?"

"I told you," I snapped, "my interest in boys is none of your business." And I angrily straightened my tunic.

"So you did," he said with a shrug, looking back down at the field. But he maintained an annoying grin. "You know, I know this boy well. I helped raise him in Castle Cove after the valiant death of his father. His father was one of the best men in my army. I think Felix is as brave as my son, Torinth. Fiercely brave, like Henri's son, Sol. Sometimes heart is better than brawn, Anna. Had Sol been here, and not busying himself with Henri in preparing for the defense of our kingdoms, perhaps he might have been fighting Marcus. Of course, Marcus is agile and a great fighter. You couldn't go wrong hanging around with any of these boys, princess. No, not wrong at all. They have the hearts of lions."

"I told you to shut up about this."

I felt like Engel, talking to him like that. But Darius seemed to bring out one's true self. He didn't act at all like a king. I think that's why I hadn't recognized him in our opening ceremony. He was so informal if not, at times, childish. I could see him using this to his advantage when dealing with his people. But those words were just plain rude.

He just raised an eyebrow.

"Sorry. I meant no disrespect, sir—"

"You're right," he said with a shrug. "Anyway, let's watch together. This should be a good match. But Onos loves Felix too. It will be hard on him, I think."

Felix put on his helm and then straightened his knee pads. Then the Imada approached center field, raising their swords.

My hands squeezed tightly. And I felt my heart trying to gallop out of my chest.

Marcus cursed under his breath. They were much too far away to hear, but I know it was something nasty. Felix offered some kind of rebuttal, probably something about the cheap shot he had dealt him during practice. It was possible his injury in practice was the real reason for the challenge.

The swords were lowered.

I could see instantly this was a good match. Both boys were highly skilled at the sword and shield, Felix being far more agile than Polius. While Marcus mirrored his father's grace, Felix overmatched him, perhaps a little, in speed. Both crashed swords against each other's shields. And it seemed Marcus hacked a little bit more than previously, probably furious over his challenged prize.

Felix kicked him, sending Marcus falling to the blue dirt. Then he rushed and pinned him. Everyone gasped. But then, as Felix drew his blade over Marcus's neck, it was quickly repelled by Marcus's shield. Incredibly, Marcus dueled while lying on the ground with Felix fighting over him. The audience and king went wild over that.

Marcus tripped him. Then they went rolling across the ground, digging up blue-brown dust over the field. Both lost their shields but held on to their swords as tightly as possible, for a lost sword meant a lost match.

"A good fight," said the king, clapping. "Marvelous!"

I nodded. He was right this time.

But then the battle became vicious. The boys began slugging each other savagely in the face with their gloved hands. One blow from Marcus, with all his weight, crashed down on poor Felix's chin. Felix closed his eyes for a moment. There was blood on Felix's face, and I wondered if Marcus had broken his jaw. But Felix wasn't done. He began trying to bring his sword down on Marcus's head and chest. If Felix could only hold the sword by Marcus's neck, that could mean a win too! But the tip of Felix's blade was unsteady. There were gasps from the crowd. Without control of Felix's sword, this was getting dangerous.

Marcus managed to hit the hilt of Felix's sword with his armored forearm. The blow threw Felix's sword from his hand.

That was it! A lost sword meant the end of a match! A cheap win for pompous Marcus.

I was mad. Victory in the games would be given to Marcus over a stupid dropped sword?

"Bravo!" cried the king. "Bravo!"

Felix crouched on his knees with his head down, trying to catch his breath, while Marcus stood over him pointing his sword at him as if Felix were a dog. Then he looked up toward me with triumph.

My mother walked down the steps yet again.

"Does anyone challenge me?" shouted Marcus, panting and standing over Felix.

It was so unfair. The sight of that conceited boy standing over poor Felix, as Felix remained on his knees, put me absolutely over the edge! If ever there should have been a victor, it should have been Felix. I had been sure Felix was going to win. If he had only not lost his grip on his sword and the battle had continued, Marcus would have lost.

So . . . I did something very stupid.

"*Aye!*" I shouted with all my might, raising my fist.

Everyone in all the rows turned and stared at me. I fought sudden overwhelming embarrassment. My face flushed. King Darius opened his eyes wider than ever.

"*I challenge you!*" I shouted, trying my best not to sound sheepish.

"You cannot," said Darius, worried. "You're not allowed, Avivae."

I ignored the king and pushed my way past him down our aisle and then rushed down the steps. Everyone's eyes were on me. Marcus looked up in amazement. My mother, who had been caught halfway down the field, stared too. Then, as I came closer, Mother gave me that same look she always did before a grave punishment.

"She's not eligible," cried Mother to the audience. "She's not allowed to compete."

But that was met by jeers.

I turned and faced the audience when I got down to the field and bowed before all my people. Then I bowed deeply before the king, whose eyes were still bulging.

"Avva!" someone shouted triumphantly. I think it was Hanna.

"That's not what the rules say," I cried. "Any man or nymph may challenge the challenger. There can be no objection. Unless Marcus wishes to forfeit."

"You disgrace Felix, princess?" jeered Marcus angrily. "Think he can't beat me, but you can?"

"It be their lands," Felix said, finally standing up. "I feel no disgrace. Let an Amazon challenge the victor upon their lands, Marcus, I say. And by the will of Persephone, I hope Princess Avivae wins."

And he came over to me, took my hand, and raised it high in the air. And at that, the stadium went crazy.

But the noise in the amphitheater didn't last long. The crowds watched as we prepared, and there was a sense of foreboding. Perhaps they were worried their princess would disgrace them? Or maybe die?

"Any man or nymph may challenge the challenger," I shouted. "Is that not true, King Darius? Is it not my right to challenge him?"

"Aye . . . it's . . . as she says," Darius said, looking away for a moment to spit on the ground. "But the queen has ordered you not to compete, Princess Avivae."

"Why, Mother?" I asked, turning to her in front of the whole kingdom. "Why can't I compete, but others who are my age fought this evening?"

"It's none of your concern."

I turned to King Darius again.

"By your own agreed-upon rules of the games, I challenge Marcus. Do you deny me this right? There is no rule dictating who the challenger is."

"I cannot deny you," he said, though every bone in his body seemed to want to say yes.

"*Darius!*" shouted my mother.

"The princess is right, Delia," shouted the king. "It's her right to challenge him."

Then it was Engel's turn to get in my way. He hobbled faster than I had ever seen his little legs go, right down the steps to the field to whisper to and advise my mother, as he did so often in the Court. And I could tell, as he kept glancing at me, that he was not advising in my favor.

But Mother pushed Engel aside and came closer to me.

"I can't allow this," she said.

I ran a hand through my long hair. Then I shook my head vehemently.

"Step away, Mother, so I may reclaim honor. Cambria lost. Marcus won. His challenger lost by dropping a sword. That was stupid. Not one of your champions has won. This is a disgrace. Allow an Amazon a victory today."

"Do not try to trick me with the honor of our people, Avivae," she hissed. "There's a good reason why I've prevented you from competing."

"Really? What?"

We were fighting. But I doubted anyone in the stadium could hear what she was saying. She was shouting her whispers at me. But Marcus heard everything.

Mother stared down into my face. She wasn't much taller anymore, but she still made me look back and meet her eyes, seeing her fury. Then she said her favorite words, which I had heard a thousand times from her.

"*How dare you!* Didn't you get enough excitement killing my mother's unicorn!"

"Is that it? I'm not competing because of what happened to Daphne?"

"No, Avivae," she blurted, putting her head in her hand. "By the gods, I thought you had left me. I thought I had lost you forever."

"And so I can't compete tonight?"

"You cannot." She raised her head and shook it. "You're too young."

"That's a lie and you know it."

I looked over at the audience. The hundreds in their benches were so quiet. Then, when I turned back, I was surprised at my mother's expression. It was different than her usual fury. She looked afraid.

"Mother, let me do this. You're right, I disgraced our family with Daphne. Let me make things right for you by winning this time."

"And if you lose? How will that give me honor? If anything happens to me, who will take my place as queen of Azure? Come on, Avva, stop being childish. Only you can twist Daphne's death into a matter of our family's honor. Go back upstairs and sit and watch Marcus have his rightful win."

"Well, Mother, if you don't let me, imagine the *dishonor* to our family now. And my embarrassment after calling out this challenge."

"*How dare you!*"

"Come fight me, princess!" Marcus said with a laugh. "Let her fight, Queen Delia. It'll be my pleasure to beat a girl."

When my mother spun around on him, even the upstart boy stumbled back.

"My queen," said Marcus, raising a hand. "I'll be quick. I won't hurt her badly. Just let her challenge me."

"Arrogant boy," Mother said, amused. "You think I don't let her fight because I fear that she will be made a fool sword fighting you?"

But he didn't dare reply.

She gazed back toward the king. Darius stood, in the crowds, where I had only a moment ago been watching the competition. He nodded. Cambria, who had been leaning on a wooden column on the sidelines, nodded too.

Mother whirled back, hating me as always.

"Suit up. Do what you need to do to meet your challenge. But don't you dare lose. And don't you dare fall like Thasius."

"Thank you, Queen Delia," I said formally with a bow.

And the crowd went wild again. They had been silent for so long, but with my bow before their queen, they went crazy.

My mother gathered the frills of her long violet dress and walked off.

"For our people, Avivae," she remarked with her back turned, leaving the field, "you better not lose."

The scarlet glistening armor brought down by Imada was heavy. Had I known I was competing, I would have brought my own fitted armor, but there was no time. My own shin and elbow guards and heavy red breast plate and torso shield were still lying in my bedchamber.

Cambria entered the field. The general herself helped me tie the iron to my body. She smiled but didn't say a word. Finally, when the heavy metal shoes, scarlet helm, red leather shin guards, elbow guards, chainmail along my shoulders and thighs, sword, and shield were readied, she patted me on my back.

"I don't think he knows what he's in for, princess," Cambria said quietly. "Neither will the rest of them. Remember what I taught you. Remember everything. But don't underestimate the general's son. He may surprise you, yet."

"Just tell me, Cambria," I said as I tied the chainmail to my waist, "did you lose on purpose?"

"General Onos is a great warrior," she said with a grin. But then she gave me a wink as she walked back to the stadium steps to stand by my mother.

My hand shook as I held the short sword. It wasn't heavy —I was just really scared. I twirled it around. Then I clutched the shield. My shield had the symbol of my people, a great multicolored phoenix, painted in the center. Marcus's shield didn't. His shield was just painted red and gold. My armor glistened scarlet. I think the Imada had rushed over the very best armor that would fit me for, truly, I was my people's champion tonight. And my people in the audience kept cheering.

But, honestly, I was scared.

I felt sweat drip down over my eyes under my helm. The helmet was someone else's, someone with a larger head. It moved around uncomfortably as I walked toward the center of the stadium.

Then I faced Marcus in center field.

The Imada lowered their swords.

"Why are you doing this, Avva?" Marcus asked, circling me. "Do you hate me this much? I thought after all we had been through, we were friends."

"I don't hate you, Marcus. I saw you that night in the Stratos. You're a good man. And a great fighter. But you cheated."

"How'd I cheat?"

"Felix told me you hurt him in practice."

"If a man's wounded in practice, he doesn't deserve to compete. That isn't cheating. There's no rule against it. Well, now I see you do hate me. But don't worry, I'll be quick. But you'll pay for embarrassing me." Then he gave an annoying smile. "Still, I can't hurt one so pretty—"

"You will lose!"

And that was it. I hacked my sword at him. The metal of our short swords clanged and rang out along the field. We dueled back and forth, parry and then thrust, back and forth, for a long time. I took this time to study his moves as one can only do during battle. He was good, quick and strong, but I believe I was faster and more agile. That was Marcus's greatest weakness. He moved slowly. But then, once I thought I had an open area to finish him, he slammed my side hard with his shield, sending me careening to the ground. Blue dust flew into my eyes. I had little time to mind it. I saw his sword coming down toward me. I quickly rolled away sideways and jumped back up and into a fighting stance again.

The crowd cheered.

"Not bad for a little girl," Marcus said, out of breath. "Not bad at all. I see you do know how to fight, Avva."

"You're not so bad . . ." I said, hacking at his shield, "yourself."

I managed to push him, then I hacked at his helm. But he blocked me with his sword. And we repeatedly crashed sword against sword.

"I shall have to show you what I showed Felix. Strength can defeat speed, Avva."

He managed to trip and throw me to the ground, rolling on me. We rolled across the field. Over and over we were spinning, just as I had seen him do with Felix. The stadium steps and the night sky spun around and around, and I became dizzy. I realized, in the recesses of my mind, that he was doing this on purpose to disorient me.

I dropped my shield, and then I grasped my sword as hard as I could. Whatever happened, I couldn't let go of my sword!

I heard gasps from the crowd. I looked over toward my mother, but that shifted my weight just enough for him to throw me on my back. With my gloved hand, I slugged him hard across his chin. I had intended on busting a lip or perhaps, even better, cutting him like he'd done to Felix. He didn't hit back. Instead, he rolled with me yet again on the ground.

By now we were panting, and I was feeling sick. No more talking. Both of us were . . . out of breath, struggling to raise our swords.

I was getting tired. If I could . . . just manage to knock his sword out of his hand, I'd win like he had. But as he slammed his shield against the arm holding my sword, I knew he had the same idea.

Back and forth, back and forth, back and forth, we rolled on the dirt, each grabbing for the other's blade. I started repeatedly hitting him hard in the face with the hilt of my sword. Most of the hits clanged his helmet, but a few landed against his cheek and forehead. He still didn't strike back.

In the frenzy, I think these were my last coherent thoughts.

I saw Hanna in the stadium. And then the king watching me. But I realized this was an illusion. All I could really see was the ground and sky spinning.

I began swooning. Marcus was gasping for air. I think he was suffering too.

We went around, turning and twisting on the hard ground for what seemed like ages. Occasionally, I'd hear the roar of the crowd burst through one ear, but then disappear and fade in the other.

I wanted it all to end. I caught a glimpse of Marcus's face. I had never seen him so angry. Now he looked like he wanted to tear me apart.

I hit his helm hard and, for a moment, his grip on me slackened and his eyes closed. It was enough for me to turn him under me. But then, just as I was about to put my sword to his neck, he opened his eyes and rolled me again. Then he groaned for a moment and seemed to let out a chuckle. He clocked me hard on the head, and everything turned dark.

When I opened my eyes, I saw the brute on top of me! His body weight pressed me into the dirt. I was pinned. He was using all of his brutish strength against me. I was finished. Defeated. I felt so much shame, and part of me just wanted to give in to my exhaustion. Still, his sword was in one hand, but he couldn't raise it over my neck for the "kill" without letting go of me.

If I was pinned long enough, the Imada might call the match! I moved again. Some cheered.

He pinned me again. But he didn't lay his sword against my neck. Rather, he did the absolutely unthinkable. In front of the entire Court, he leaned down and kissed me on the lips.

Laughter ran through the stadium. I thought of my mother and the king and Engel looking down on me as a complete fool. But my shame sparked just enough rage for me to jolt my hips and force him to fall on his side. I had to push hard, for the boy was heavy, but I managed to turn him. My throw enabled me to quickly spread my legs over his and point the tip of my blade at his throat. I was so mad, I had to force myself to not stick it through his neck. Then I was as surprised by the outcome as the audience was. The cheers were deafening.

I won!

"Not fair!" cried Marcus under me. "Not fair!"

He tugged off his helm. I didn't kiss him back—I hit him with my gloved fists right across his face. Then I rose, removed my helm, and bowed before King Darius.

The king was beside himself, jumping up and down and hollering with more excitement than I had ever seen before. Then came my mother, and Engel behind her, rushing across the field to me. Mother smiled, and her smile was real. I had never seen her look so proud of me. She took me into her arms and hugged me in front of the whole crowd, making the crowd go wilder. Then Marcus, the loser, bowed deeply before me and my mother.

"I concede her win," Marcus said. "You deserve it, Princess Anne."

My mother laid the crown of leaves upon my head. As if in a dream, I was in disbelief over my triumph. But there I stood, representative of both kingdoms, the victor among all the soldiers my age.

I had returned my people's honor and received a great honor myself. And, for the first time in my life, I truly felt like a queen.

11

───────

FELIX

I HAD TOLD FELIX TO MEET ME BY THE MAZE AFTER SUPPER, right? Well, that was vague. I wondered if he knew where the entrance to the maze was. He said he'd seen the maze, I think.

I hadn't eaten much at supper. That had been stupid because my stomach was growling, and I felt like I could eat the small green birds chirping on the tree branches above me. Hanna always said I didn't eat a very healthy diet. I had kinda always viewed eating as a chore. Well, I was really hungry now. But I wasn't going to go there looking and smelling like I did after my match with Marcus. So I had spent a long time in my bedchamber combing my annoying curls and applying the perfect blush and eye makeup to my face and picking the finest oils so I'd smell nice. Of course, my hair wouldn't do. It would never do. No matter how many strokes I gave it with my brush it never looked right. So, I'd wash my face and hair in a basin in my bedchamber and start everything all over again.

I wore a lovely azure dress, the color of the land—as my mother was prone to do. It ran from my neck, with a tall collar —which was the royal fashion of the Court—down to the pretty white silk and lace cuffs along my wrists. This was not a peplos, as was the fashion outside of Azurea. It was a formal long-sleeved Amazon dress. But I wore sandals to make it look less formal.

I missed Hanna. She could have braided my hair and made me laugh talking about how cute Felix was. And he was so handsome.

I supposed I was a little quick to fight with Hanna. That was stupid. I resolved to apologize to her the moment I returned to the palace. She could believe whatever she'd like about Daphne, for all I cared.

Now, sitting at the maze entrance, I kept my hands between my legs, my fingers fidgeting, as I straightened on the wooden bench, like Engel had always taught me to do. And then I waited.

And waited. Waited some more . . . Soon, I began to worry that I was being stood up. That was dumb. I had probably come too early, and he was probably still at supper.

That's when he arrived. He was dressed up too, wearing a princely brown tunic and pants, slicked-back blond hair, and very nice boots. I barely recognized him. And those pimples, those awful messes on his forehead, were covered with makeup. But he couldn't cover up the recent savage gash and bruising along his cheek and chin, no matter how hard he tried. He had bruises all over his face from that brute Marcus.

"Good evening, Princess Avivae," he said with a bow. Then he reached out his hand for mine to kiss. I giggled and handed it to him, and he kissed it.

"Stop it," I said, laughing. "Stop being so formal, Felix. You're being ridiculous."

"May I sit with you?"

Of course he may. That's why I was on a bench that fit two behinds.

He obliged and sat down. Then he made me happier than you can possibly imagine by opening a box with two honey cakes.

"I didn't see you at supper so I thought you might be hungry. Of course, it's your food from Azurea. We didn't bring much food from home. Are you hungry?"

"I sure am!" I said, snatching a cake.

He laughed. I didn't care that some of the sugar might get all over my best dress. I was famished. I think he was going to eat the other one, but after watching me, he handed me that one too. And all the while, he just sat enjoying our palace garden, gazing at the perfectly manicured blue-green and red bushes, violet birds, and glowing blue butterflies—things, I have heard, that are not found in his yellow lands.

"Avva, congratulations on your win. It was well deserved."

"He's a brute, isn't he? He didn't deserve to beat you. A lost sword was so unfair."

He nodded.

Then I gazed at his face again. He had tried to cover all those scratches and bruises. I hadn't come out of the battle with half as many injuries. Apparently, the two boys had spent more time boxing each other's faces. Marcus hadn't even hit my face. In a way, that was as chivalrously stupid as his infernal kiss.

I reached up to touch Felix's chin. His gash looked awful.

Then I humiliated myself. The finger I used had a little yellow frosting on it.

At first he moved back, surprised. But I kept trying to take the frosting off, and he kept moving away.

"What are you doing?" he asked, laughing.

"I got some on your face." He stopped and I was readying my white cloth to wipe off the frosting. "I'm sorry, how embarrassing."

But he snatched my hand and touched the frosting himself. He was such a gentle boy that his reflexes surprised me.

"I was wondering if I'd get to have a taste," he said, licking his finger.

I laughed.

"It's very good," he said, licking some more and chuckling. Then he leaned back and just looked about him again. "Ah, Anne, you are as radiant as your palace. Thank you for joining me tonight."

"I'm glad I did. You brought the most delicious food."

"Good." But then he paused and looked down pensively. "There's something that's been bothering me. It's been on my mind all evening. Did you fight Marcus over me? After I lost the match?"

"Yes. I told you, I thought it was unfair. They should never have given him the win over a lost sword."

He didn't like that. I wondered if it was because I was a girl? I'd learned men outside of Azure thought like that. To make him feel better, I said, "But it wasn't only for you, Felix, it was for our people. His father had just beaten our best general. And, anyway, I thought *you* had challenged him for *me*. Did you?"

"Aye," he said with a grin. But then he shook his head. "No, not really. Well, if I had thought it would draw me closer to the princess, indeed, I would have fought Marcus for you."

"Why did you do it then?"

"Aside from war, the games are the only way for us to prove ourselves. I was embarrassed by my quick defeat. Then I was as mad about losing over a lost sword as you were. You see, when Father died, I swore I'd be the best soldier in the Sun Kingdom. Marcus is one of our best. I thought beating him would make me one of the best too."

"You are, Felix."

"Anna, I lost. To both of you, it seems. Seems I'm not as good a soldier as you either."

"No, you have heart, Felix. You're a better man. That makes you better in battle. The king hinted as much to me when we watched you."

He scooted closer to me over that. Then he gazed at me

with his light-blue eyes. Those adorable eyes. I turned away, embarrassed a little. But my heart beat faster in my chest.

"You know," he said with a little sadness in his eyes, "I will never forget this night with the princess of Azure. But, I have to say——"

"There you go being formal again."

"Let me finish, Avva."

Well, I finished my cake. And then I licked my fingers. It was delicious.

I didn't let him keep talking. I was too excited to show him the gardens.

"Come on! Let me take you around our zoo, Felix. Even at night, we have the torches to light up everything. I'm sure you'd like to see our animals?"

We walked along a beautiful stone path through the blue-green grass. To my left, down a grassy hill, were trickling streams and waterfalls running down to the walls of our Crystal Palace. And we passed many other buildings along the garden walkway, like our great throne room, that were made of glass too. Around us under the moonlight, I could just see the white shimmer from all the walls of glass. It is said that the Mandrigel, Engel's people, once built the palace out of an ancient fortress. They adorned all the walls with crystal. Of course, midday, under the green sun, the castle shone a wonderous emerald. But under the moonlight now, everything was lit bright white. I talked about our palace with Felix as we walked.

We didn't go into the maze, but we looked at the walls of blue and purple hedges near us as we walked the paths. I remembered, with amusement, snooping around just a couple weeks ago with Hanna and listening to Andalay talk about the very boy I was with tonight. I wondered what Andalay would have thought if she saw me walking with her love interest now. And we passed small streams through perfectly manicured blue-green hedges and lovely trickling water. The garden grounds were so lovely.

There were a few other nymphs out and about this evening; usually, there were far more. The evening meal included another dance tonight. All the nymphs that passed congratulated me. Then they looked with amusement at Felix.

The zoo was a single-room cottage among thick trees with a worn thatched roof. Inside were two rows of metal cages. We perused the animals in the cages. I didn't have much interest, really, I visited all the time. And it was a bit smelly. But Felix's eyes bulged in wonder at these animals. There were red and purple birds, lapis deer, and indigo snakes. Only creatures found in Azure were in the cages. It made me think of how interesting it would be to visit a zoo in his yellow lands one day.

All these animals didn't interest him as much as the sound of a growl. At the end of the building prowled our zaffre tiger in the largest cage. This beast was the size of a man. He was purple with black stripes and huge jaws, moving slowly about, with his eyes turning white in the glare of the flickering torches lining the wooden walls.

"Come on, let me show you my absolute favorite," I said, pulling at his arm. He nodded but still stared back at the tiger.

"That's a baby, you know."

"*A baby!*"

"Aha," I said with a laugh. "Zaffre tigers grow two times that size. But they're rarely seen. They know how to hide so well, even from our best hunters. Cambria told me they'd release that one when it grew too large."

"Have you seen them in the wild, Anne?"

I loved how he called me Anne. No one ever called me Anne, my name pronounced in Atalan, except Felix and the king. I also would have loved it more if he had held my hand. Instead, he walked close to me.

I led him to the last cage. My favorite. There a large,

majestic black bird with rainbow-tipped feathers and tail, a red and blue chest, and an azure patch on his head perched on a branch. I grabbed Felix by the shoulder. (He still kept staring back at the tiger.)

"What sort of bird is this, Anna?"

"A phoenix. Said to be the only one. It's my people's bird. It is—"

"Aye, I see it on your shields and on your flag. He looks almost like our hawks back home, but so much larger. And blacker and with feathers so wonderful and colorful."

"They say he's immortal, Felix. I—" I looked around. "I should have planned this. Darn it. One of our zookeepers could have opened the cage. He's really tame and I love petting his wings. Some say he knew the great Queen Nephratee and even Queen Harmonia."

"He almost looks as if he doesn't belong in a cage."

"But isn't he beautiful?"

Felix looked right into my eyes when I said that. And I kind of meant *isn't Felix beautiful?* And then, just like at our impromptu meeting at lunch, we just sort of stared into each other's eyes.

"Beautiful," he muttered with a nod.

Of course, now would have been the perfect time to kiss me. All he had to do is lean down and. . . I mean, Marcus, that jerk, did it in front of the whole sarding kingdom.

He didn't do it. Boys will be boys, I suppose.

"Are you sore, Anna?" he asked, lightly touching my bruised neck.

"A little. But I've gotten far worse. Cambria is pretty brutal, a lot more dangerous than Marcus. I once thought I'd never make it through one of her lessons. Once I even broke an arm, and Engel and the queen were so mad. But Cambria told them I had to learn."

"Onos is the same," Felix said with a nod. "He always tells us that if we don't hurt, we haven't fought hard enough. That wasn't my first match with Marcus. We've trained together. Believe it or not, we're friends. We hate and like each other. We're competitive, but when we face the enemy, he's the best friend anyone could have."

I nodded. I could certainly imagine that.

Then we just stood there. Both uncomfortable, standing in front of our magnificent phoenix. It really wasn't about the bird anymore. It was about my urge to hold his hand, or . . . do something else, you know. But . . . nothing happened.

I touched his hand and he rubbed my fingers.

Then he turned me toward him. He seemed nervous, but he became transfixed by my eyes again.

And then, he finally leaned down. He reached out slowly and touched his lips so gently to mine. It was meant to be gentle but, actually, it was a bit clumsy. But nice. Not vulgar like Marcus. So nice.

"Sweet," I said. "That was so sweet, Felix."

"Not as sweet as you, princess."

I turned from him, but he gently turned me back, leaning down again. He was going to try for another kiss.

But then the phoenix flew straight into the bars of the cage, ruffling his feathers like crazy.

"*Has he gone mad?!*" cried Felix.

I lost control of myself, laughing.

"What's so funny?"

"That bird is a lot smarter than he lets on. I don't think he likes you kissing me."

"A thousand pardons," he said with a bow to the bird.

"I liked it."

"You did?"

"Let's go in the maze," I said with a nod, rubbing his hand. "Let me show you. There are torches lighting every turn. We can get lost in the maze together."

12

HANNA

"*You kissed Felix!*" exclaimed Hanna with bulging shiny blue eyes.

We were in my bedchamber, and I was performing my usual task, brushing the knots out of my hair beside my large mirror. I knew she couldn't help herself with gossip, but I had to be careful. Just yesterday, she had told me that she fancied him. Remember? It seemed like during the whole festival we had kept vying for the same man.

"You know, Hanna," I said, looking at myself in my mirror, "we have to be schooled next week. Our break is over."

"Maybe we can ditch Engel," she said with a chuckle. Then she grabbed my arm and said, "Never mind. Tell me, tell me everything that happened. How did it happen? Where?"

"Well, I mean, we're friends now."

"Felix?"

"Yes. He's a really nice boy. Andalay was right about him."

"Nobody said he isn't nice. But . . . stop combing!" She grabbed my shoulder and spun me around hard. "Stop ignoring me and tell me all about it. You kissed him?"

"There's not much to tell," I said with a laugh. "He's kind of cute under all those pimples. Anyway, we met at the maze."

"He *is* cute, Blue. He's really handsome."

"We're just friends," I said and brushed my hair again. "It's nothing. You can see him off at the Strait if you want."

"It's okay," she said, putting a hand on my arm. "I was just getting over Marcus. I really don't even know him. And I don't blame you for Daphne. Oh, Avva, all our fighting is stupid."

I cocked my head and raised an eyebrow.

"But tell me about Felix."

After more laughing, I told her. I told her all about my evening. She sat in a chair and just listened as I gave her all the juicy details while combing my hair. When I got to the *kiss*, she just about died.

"*Friends*, Avva?"

"Honestly Hanna, yes, I think just friends. And he's a good friend. He's so nice."

Just then, while I was pulling out a particularly nasty knot, Engel came hobbling into my room. He didn't knock. He just barged through the door like he always did. I needed to find a lock or something.

"Don't forget about tonight, Avva," Engel said. "You're to dine alone with the king and your mother at supper."

"And you?"

"I might be there."

"Hmm, you're always there. I can't seem to get rid of you."

"Just come down. And dress well. Kind of like the way you dressed for that boy last night." And he laughed and snorted.

"How'd you know about last night?"

"The palace isn't large," Engel said. Then he winked.

"Please, leave me alone, Engel."

"Just don't be late." Then Engel turned to Hanna and nodded. "Hi, Hanna."

"Don't bother saying hi to her. She knows you don't really care about her. And next time, try knocking."

"Good day, Hanna," he said. Then he turned around and hobbled out. "You can tell me all about Felix later, Avva."

"Engel, she took him to the maze," hollered Hanna stupidly, "and she said she kissed him!"

"I heard," Engel said, now walking down the hall. "The whole kingdom heard."

"*Ooooh!*" That made me angry. I threw down the brush and looked at Hanna. "What does he mean, the whole kingdom? He can be so irritating."

"Avva?" Hanna said, touching my shoulder.

"Yeah? What?"

"Can I braid your hair?"

13

THE GREAT DECEPTION

I wore the same dress I had worn for Felix. It was not only very pretty, it was also very comfortable. Then I walked down the royal halls and past our great lookout. This lookout was the greatest place in the whole palace with two large spiral staircases made of marble and a huge two- to three-story wall of glass. At the top of these stairs, I could just look out on the whole kingdom, and, if I looked far enough, I could see the yellow lands across the Strait in the distance. I had seen the shore so many times before, but now, as all the men were sailing away, the thought of glimpsing their home made me feel a little sad. As I descended the spiral stairs, I kept glancing out that giant window. But I couldn't see the sea now, there was too much of a blue haze. At the bottom of the stairs two sentries in scarlet hoplite armor stood at attention. The guards had stood like that for centuries, guarding the bedchambers of the royal Ambrosia family. I knew both these two nymphs well —Casia and Elpis—and it seemed like they wanted to wave at me as I headed down another hallway to our grand dining room, but they had been trained to stand still when standing guard.

I was late. Again.

I entered an oak-walled dining room, the one I had eaten breakfast in on our second day with our guests. Remember? Where Marcus passed that stupid note asking to meet me at the bridge.

Inside the large hall a giant wooden table ran almost the entire length of the large room. And at the very end sat my mother with the king. And Engel, the wonderful little purple man.

"Anna!" cried the king with his usual exuberance, standing up.

He wore a long purple robe with a frilly white collar. His long black hair was slicked back. He had many golden rings on his fingers and wore a large necklace of gems and rubies. If ever he looked like a king, it was tonight. Mother did not rise. She sat beside him nodding, wearing a very lovely white dress with a large collar up to her ears. Her dark hair was combed back. Sometimes I marveled at how beautiful that witch could look. I couldn't get too mad at her appearance, I supposed. So many said she and I resembled one another.

Then, as I made my way down the long aisle of wooden chairs, I tried not to laugh at Engel. He was formal too, wearing a large collar, white tunic, and black pants. He was dressed a little like the king.

"Have a seat, Anna," King Darius said, gesturing across from him. Mother was at the head of the table. I sat facing Engel and the king. Behind them, windows looked out at our palace gardens.

A large cornucopia had already been laid on the table: fruits, breads, dates, figs, cherries, olives, cheeses, pheasant, and beef, and anything else you could desire or imagine. Engel was stuffing his plate.

"Must you call her Anna?" asked my mother, rolling her eyes. "Her name is Avivae."

"It's how we say it, dear. Sorry. Would you like me to call her Anne?"

I chuckled. It seemed this king liked a good fight with Mother too. She merely grunted and then raised her crystal glass of wine before me.

"Be a dear, Darius, and pour some myrle berry wine for her," Mother said with a smile. "Just a little for this special occasion. A toast to my daughter. The actions of Avivae have indeed honored Azurea and all my Amazons. She has honored all of us."

Well, that's something new. I don't remember a time when Mother congratulated me for anything. Honestly, I don't recall her smiling at me much either.

King Darius obliged with a nod. It was funny to watch him serving me with all his ornate clothes. But he did it with such gusto and a big grin, as usual. Where did this king get all his energy?

"Now raise your glass, my child," said my mother.

I obliged.

"To Princess Avivae." She raised her glass. "To my daughter. You have been a very naughty girl, driving me and Engel mad, but your actions in the game were exemplary. Your win was glorious, particularly with Onos's son's behavior being so improper. And it deserves payment by your king and queen."

"Must you talk to me like I'm one of your subjects?"

"I'm trying to give you a compliment." But I was beginning to want to just drink the myrle berry wine.

"Let me just say it then, shall I, Avivae?" Mother continued. "I'm proud of you. You proved yourself an Ambrosia yesterday and a princess. I've decided to not punish you anymore for what happened to dear Daphne. Her fate has undoubtedly been hard enough on you. Not only that, I shall not ground you in flight this year. You may tend unicorns again, and I will give you Naya to fly as your own."

"We're very proud of you," chimed in the king, nodding.

"We're proud of you, Blue," echoed Engel with a big grin, raising his own glass.

"Thanks," I said with a shrug. Then I sipped some wine. The pomegranate wine was sweet, but sharp.

"But," the king said, suddenly turning serious, "we need to talk about something important before I leave."

I tore off some bread. I might as well eat if he had something important to say. Then I gathered a bunch of olives in my hand. With a mouth full of olives, I asked, "What?"

All three of them raised their crystal glasses to me again. That was nice. I drank a little more, too—particularly since I usually wasn't permitted to drink wine.

"You need me to go hunting with Cambria to get rid of more of those amphiuma, or something?" I asked with my mouth full. "I'd be glad to do it."

"Cambria's already taken care of the vermin," Mother said. "But we're proud of that too."

Then she pushed her dish to the side. It must be really important.

"Is it about Felix?" I asked, looking over at Engel. I felt myself blush a little.

"It is a little like that," the king said with a chuckle. "Because, as you know, Felix is leaving tomorrow too."

"Is it about you and my mother, sir?"

The king solemnly nodded.

"I see how you two get along. Are you planning on getting married?"

They looked at each other. What were they trying to say? They should have just come out and said it already.

The king said, "Avva, do you remember what we spoke of during the games? You asked me about the state of my kingdom. The state of the continent of Atala and the Sun Kingdom."

"No, sir, I don't remember."

"You asked me if you were safe. A smart question for a young lady that's obviously no longer a girl."

"Are we?"

I didn't like the way the queen and king looked at each other over that.

"Your father is a powerful king and a mighty warrior," my mother said. "But times have become so dangerous that your father's army may not be able to hold back the enemy. It's possible that these games are in preparation for something far more terrible. Did you notice that no other kingdom participated in the games this Olympiad? This is a first in centuries for Azure Blue. Your father's Sun Kingdom and Napea are working together, now in games, perhaps later in battle to protect Northern Atala. To protect all of the continent of Atala."

I dropped my food. I think I was staring at her, like Hanna often did, with my mouth open like a fish. I hadn't heard half of what she had said, nor had I really cared. It was something about politics and this and that and whatever. But it was the word *father*, which she kept repeating, that got my attention. And she kept saying it. *"Your father did this, and then your father did that."* That's all I heard. *Father. Father. Father.* I had been told since I was little that my father had died after mother met him in the games.

"This is difficult," the king said, rubbing his eyes.

"Darius, we agreed to do this tonight," said my mother, raising a hand to him. Then she turned to me again. "Avva, don't ask any questions until I'm done speaking. All right?"

I couldn't say a word. Wouldn't dare. But I felt my face warming up.

"Your father is the mightiest king in all of Atala." There she was, at it again. "He's a just ruler, kind but stern. Your father protects our lands and—"

"What do you mean, *father!* Why do you keep saying that? Are. . . are you two getting married? Is that it?"

They shook their heads.

"Mother, you told me my father was killed by Poseidon? It was after meeting you in Azure as he traveled back across the

Strait to return home from the games four Olympiads ago. You said a great tempest appeared across the water and he drowned. Engel told me he was once a great king in Southern Atala." Engel looked down. "But neither he nor you ever hinted that he could still be alive."

"I asked that you not interrupt me. Do you obey anything I ask anymore, Avivae?"

"But how can you drop the word *father* and expect me not to say anything?" I looked at all three of them. They looked dreadful. Then I squinted my eyes and glared at her. "Just say what you need to say, instead of hinting. Stop this formal babble for once, Mother. What about *Father*?"

"Please, Anna," said the king gently. "Please listen and then you will know."

"Sir," I said, facing the king, "is she referring to you? I asked if you two intended to get married? Is she referring to you now as my father because after marrying her, I will be your daughter?"

"No," he said, shaking his head.

"Then what is this about?"

"Won't you let me finish?" asked Mother.

They seemed sad. *Why?*

But then she didn't finish. She just quickly turned to her crystal glass of myrle berry wine and drank more. I noticed her hand shaking as she sipped the wine. Then she put the glass down and folded her hands, leaning forward and speaking gruffly. "Avivae… let me try this another way. You know this is the first time we've had the games in the winter. That was all done so that your … *father* … could come to our lands before the start of war. War is inevitable. It will happen, and so King Darius and I decided to move the games."

"I understand, Mother. That way he could see you. So you are marrying him then?"

"No," she said, shaking her head. "He didn't come here to see me. He came to see *you*. King Darius came to see his daughter. You were conceived with him. We were already married fourteen years ago when I conceived you."

I don't know how I can explain how those words made me feel. In some ways, I was happy. I liked this king a lot. If ever I wanted anyone to be my father, my real father, it would be him. But then there was a feeling of deception. Of lies. Why had I not been told before? Anyone growing up with only one parent wonders about the other, even dreams of one day seeing the other. Even if as a ghost or apparition, I would have died to have met my real father. But now, as he sat before me, I found I was as tongue-tied as they were. It was a complete shock, and all three of them looked like they were trying to be so careful, as if I were a zaffre tiger who had been let loose upon the dining hall and they were hiding to avoid being eaten. Engel dipped his head down, the queen looked out one of the windows, into the foggy darkness, and the king—my *father!?*—rubbed his hand over his eyes and through his long beard nervously.

"Tomorrow he has to leave, Avva."

"*How dare you!*" I shouted with the same venom she had always given me. I leaped up. "*Do you enjoy watching me suffer? How can you tell me this and then tell me he has to leave!*"

"He has to leave in order to protect our kingdom, princess."

"Why?"

"Let me finish, Avva. Neither our land nor his accepts you as his daughter. In our lands, the truth of your father and my past would destroy the royal families. And in your father's lands, nymphs aren't considered human. You wouldn't be accepted as a princess in Azerban."

"*How could you keep such a secret from me?*" I shouted. I whirled around at Engel. The dwarf had sunken in his chair, looking faint. "*How could you do this to me! And why are you all telling me now? You waited until all the men were in their ships so I—*" I started choking up. "*So gossip wouldn't spread about the king's nymph daughter in Azerban? Is that it?*"

"Anna," said the king. "Our situation is difficult. You have to listen—"

"*I don't even know who you are, sir!*"

And that seemed to kill the king. He quickly turned and looked out the window into darkness, at nothing at all.

Then my mother, typically formal, stated the well-known edict set by Nephrea and Hades, the god of the underworld: "*Any outworlder who steps foot on Gaia will come to me.*"

"*I am well aware of that sarding edict, Mother!*"

"Then you must be equally aware, child, that the penalty for breaking the law is an end of our immortality. I broke that edict and fell in love with your father, King Darius, outside of Azure. Therefore, it is only a matter of time until I will be taken down. That is why I did not let you compete in the games. There must be a successor for the Amazons. Nothing can happen to you, or there will be no more Ambrosia line. And that is why I did not permit you—"

"*What does that have to do with not telling me?*"

"I broke the edict, Avivae!" she cried, slapping the table with her palm. "I will die. The gods have given me mercy, bartered with me, for time for you to grow and take my place! Only through my libations and penitence, my submission to their orders, to our edicts, and to the power of our Elders and the Imada, and my begging the god of the Underworld, Hades, to accept my rites to Cora, the goddess Persephone, have I not been taken down before you were grown! I angered the gods, but Hades sent me mercy! I pointed out the lack of justice that had befallen my own mother in Colchis! Hades still called me damned. All I could do after my transgression was beg for a life long enough to pass on my rule to you before my departure. Not to the Elders, Avivae. But to *you*. When I pass, Avivae, you will be crowned queen. And now, with the things you proved at the games, you will be ready. Then I shall be taken down by Hades to the underworld and—"

"*You deserve it!*"

"That's not the point!" she shouted back, jumping up. But then she put her head in her hand, taking a deep breath. "Don't you see, I couldn't tell our people about you and your father. We kept the secret for the people."

"Why?"

"Are you an idiot?" asked my mother, glaring at me. And although she held her usual fury, I saw tears forming in her eyes. The king tried to ease her by placing a hand on her arm, but she shook it off. "If the people knew what we had done, they'd be furious. *I* can cross the Strait, but our people cannot? What would this do to our kingdoms? To the people, Avivae?"

"So you deceived them too? You lied to our people and me?"

"Stop it, Blue," Engel said. "This is tearing them apart."

"Shut up, Engel! What gives you the right to even be here! You knew this all along too?"

"He has every right," said my infernal mother. "He raised you."

"So I've heard. Because of the same queen, Nephratee, who established that sarding rule and forced you to not tell me who *my real father was!*"

"We have to follow the laws of the land, Avivae," she said with a sigh. Then she fell back in her chair. "We must follow the gods' rule. Amazons practice no rites to the gods, as decreed, except—during the games—to Nephratee's favorite, Persephone. And even Cora was abandoned by Zeus. We give no libations to any other god. The Amazon are in great danger due to our hubris. We—"

Her hypocrisy stung my ears. I stopped listening and had a sudden urge to run out of the room. I turned to the king. His tender smile—my *father's* smile, my actual, *real* father—made me even angrier. This kindness could have been mine all my life. That love, instead of this terrible woman's, could have been mine since I was a baby. And now, my father was leaving? He had entered my life for one evening to announce that he'd be gone.

"Well, Father, you can go now," I shouted to the king. "Now that you've seen me, told me who you are, why not go home!"

And that was it. I ran out of the room in tears.

14

BEING BLUE

So my father is King Darius of the Sun Kingdom. I found that out right before he sets sail to leave me for good. Some father. And some mother, who decides to never tell me until it's too late. He seems like a good man. Of course, I'll never know because he'll be heading back across the Strait of Azure to his castle in Azerban. I can't visit him either, of course, because of Nephratee's edict forbidding any nymph from crossing. And so, I'll just sit here in my misery, as always, cataloging it all. Why did they even bother to tell me!

I HEARD a knock on the door. So I stopped writing on the parchment.

"Go away, please."

"Princess, it's me." It was Engel's voice. Of course, it was Engel. It was always Engel there to comfort me. Never my mother… or my *father.*

"Go away."

"Princess, just open the door."

"Really, Engel, I'm surprised you don't just barge in. That's what you always do."

And then that's precisely what the dwarf did. He opened the latch on the door and hobbled in. I quickly rolled up the parchment and turned my back on him, still sitting on my chair before my desk.

"Blue, you're being blue again."

"Go away."

"Blue."

"My name is Avivae Ambrosia. I am the princess of Azure, daughter of Delia Ambrosia and King Darius. What is my father's last name, anyway?"

"Solinaray."

"Then I am also Avivae Solinaray."

Engel chuckled. I did too, in spite of myself.

"That's better, princess," he said, walking to the edge of the bed. "At least you still have your sense of humor."

But then I fell apart. I cried and cried in my hands. I felt him jump on the bed and lean his head onto my shoulder, comforting me as he always had. I think Engel cried too.

"I'm sorry, Avva. I'm so sorry for not being able to tell you. I wanted to for so many years."

"It's not you, Engel. It's them. They're so horrible."

He leaned into me, gently kissing me on the cheek. Then he said, "I am so proud of you. In a fortnight, you survived the forest alone and championed the queen. You gave honor to our people. Had my greatest friend, Nephrea, still been alive, I can tell you, she would have been so proud of who you are. You are what your mother said you are, truly the princess of Azure."

"I don't care, Engel," I said between sobs. "I killed Daphne."

But that was a terribly sad thing to say. Engel loved Daphne too.

"Oh Avva," Engel said, "you complain that your mother is cruel to you. Why torture yourself now?"

Wise Engel. Sweet Engel. My confidant and closest friend.

That man, that kind king downstairs in the dining hall, he was not really my father. Engel was. So I just melted in the dwarf's arms and cried for the longest time.

"Daphne loved you, Avva," he said softly.

"I know, Engel. I know. I watched her save my life."

I leaned back and he used a stubby purple finger to clear a tear from my eye.

"Oh, Avva, life is so hard. Try not to make it worse by hurting yourself. There's still supper downstairs. Come down."

"I don't want to eat."

"I really wasn't talking about food. All this pains the king, probably a lot more than it pains you. He agreed with your mother on the deception for the benefit of our kingdoms, but his heart never agreed to it. He fought her many times over it. Now he just wants to say goodbye. I think you should see him before he goes."

I jumped up.

I walked to my window. It was raining gently outside. That made it gloomier. I could not see the stars through the clouds. And there was no way I could make out the sea in the distance through all the mist. That was probably best.

"Engel? You seem to know this king so well. How? How do you know him?"

"We're friends, Blue," he said. "I met him with your mother. He came with a great delegation across the sea to discuss a treaty between our people. It was the first time since Dainya's time that such a meeting had been called with Hinterland men and our Elders. Just like at the games, a group of a hundred men crossed the Strait by sail and met in the fields before the palace. There the king and your mother discussed a treaty between the lands of the Shadow Forest, Azerban, and Napea. And then, in the course of deliberations, your mother and the king fell in love. How could they not? They're both strong, competitive, willful people. He only stayed for a half fortnight, according to your mother's own edict. But for many moons afterward, all I heard from the queen was words about him. *"Do you think he's handsome, Engel? Do you think he likes me?"* We laughed. *"What was he wearing, it's been so long I can barely even remember! He had long, wavy black hair, didn't he? Such broad shoulders and a man with bounding energy.* And on and on. Of course, she had fallen in love with him. I've been around long enough to have seen it before. I watched it happen to Nephrea and Dainya. At first, perhaps they only had a crush. But then the crush never ended, Avva."

"What happened then?" I leaned my forehead against the window, still listening. I loved it when Engel told me stories.

"Well, with so much interest, do you think, Avva, that letters were enough for your mother? The only way, of course, was to break her own law—Nephrea's edict. Your mother, a rule follower like your grandmother, had to break her own rules to see Darius. She had to cross the Strait in secret. She hadn't been naughty since she was your age, and her violations had been minor. Crossing the Strait was, of course, our people's greatest offense. I argued for her not to do it, pleading with her to not make this mistake. I knew this would lead to her being taken from me to the underworld. But she insisted. She said immortality was an easy trade for love. I thought about that for a while and . . . I didn't disagree."

"I see."

"Do you? You see, Avva, you feel pain because you didn't know your father, but imagine what your mother has felt all these years not being able to see him. Or your father, who hasn't seen you much since news of your birth? Only on the last few Olympiads for a handful of days. And only for half a fortnight . . ."

"She could've told me. She and Father could have trusted that I wouldn't tell."

"Maybe. You weren't to be told until you were old enough. She didn't tell anyone except her Court adviser—me—and the Elders. If it had been up to the Elders, you would never have known. She still hesitated to tell you today, but the king and I explained that you didn't deserve this deception any longer, especially with the honor and victory you handed our people." I was angry again over that. Engel noticed and quickly added, "Avva, you have to understand that even if we had told you before, you wouldn't have been able to see him anyway."

"Why?"

I sluggishly returned to my bed. Then I sat down and hung my head. He climbed up and put a hand on my shoulder.

"See your father before he goes. He really needs you now, Blue. He likes you so much."

"He seems like a good man."

"He's the best of men. Not only does Delia work with him because of their love, she works with the king out of respect."

"He's better than her."

"Now, that's not fair," Engel said, wagging a finger. "The queen does everything for Azure Blue and our people. She follows the rules given her when she was born. If you understand that, one day, you might forgive her."

"So, everything is well, then? So, I can wave goodbye to my father and never see him again?"

"Oh, Blue, please, try to look at things more clearly. Your parents have done everything they can for you. They love you. Please try to forgive their failures."

I shrugged my shoulders. "You didn't seem to like him much when Thasius died."

"We're friends. We fight like family, but he and I will always be the best of friends, Avva. For me, please say goodbye to him. Not only is he the fairest, strongest king of all the lands, but he has a huge heart. And he loves you, Avva. But now his heart, I'm afraid, is broken."

I walked back down to the dining room in a long mauve nightgown. It was quiet. Most everyone in the palace was asleep. When I opened the door, Mother wasn't there. Only King Darius. He sat near the head of the table. I didn't think he had ever changed seats. But his wooden chair was turned, and he was staring out the window looking terribly depressed —so different, so different from his usual exuberant self.

But he smiled when I walked in.

"It's funny, Anne," he said with a smile as I took a seat, "your mother and I've written so many letters and daydreamed for many moons about finally seeing each other, but now that the final night has arrived, we wish to be left alone."

"You should go see her. You should go visit her tonight."

"You think so? I don't think so."

"Why are you so sad?" I asked. But my voice cracked too. It seemed the question was meant for both of us.

"I think you know," he said, raising a finger. "I'm so proud of you. You have the best traits of your mother. I have no doubt you will make a fine Amazon Queen for Napea."

"I'd rather stay a princess."

"Really?" he asked with a chuckle. "That was the opposite of what you said when I first met you at the games this Olympiad. All you wanted to do was to be a woman. Please, sit with me, Anne. Spend time with me. Tell me of that boy. . . Felix, was it?"

"I told you, I don't want to talk about boys." But I smiled.

There was still a plate of food on the table. He gently offered it to me. I realized that with all the excitement, I hadn't eaten much. Some celebratory dinner.

He sipped wine. And then he examined the crystal glass.

"Myrle berry wine in a crystal glass. You know, Anne, this is like your land, so sweet and special. Treasure it. This is like a wondrous ruby, a treasure so wondrous in my lands of Gaia back home. We have no pomegranate wine back home. We don't even have crystal glasses. No glass windows. Our world is nothing like yours."

"So, you'll give me some more?"

He laughed and nodded. He poured me a little from a crystal pitcher. Just a little.

Then we just turned morose and quiet. I didn't totally mind. I liked just sitting there and looking outside. The clouds were dispersing a little, and I could make out stars.

"Are we safe?" I asked, breaking the silence.

"I do not know," he said, shaking his head and looking at the wine glass again. "I really don't know, Anna. I know your mother and I will do all we can to defend our kingdoms, but no one can predict the future. Well, Henri, my wizard, has some gifts of prophecy. He claims very good things for you." He smiled again, sipping more wine. "Perhaps with Onos and Henri, we stand a chance against Morteus and the Crystal Kingdom. But, by the gods, we fight Hades himself, I think. Of course, Henri didn't tell me many details, but he said that if we must fight, Azure will join us. And then, one day, Azure would see peace again. And he spoke of my daughter Anna Ambrosia being a part of that peace. I think all we can do is live. Fight like you did against the amphiuma with Marcus—" And then he smiled a sly smile and winked. "And live as you spent time with Felix."

"My stupidity killed Daphne."

"Yes, it did," he said. But then he quickly added, "But, perhaps, it was that steed's time to go, Anna. I saw that unicorn last time I visited the stables. I saw her with you. I'm not so sure such a legend was happy being locked in a tower stable. I think you set her free."

Then he smiled sadly. And it wasn't my tears I saw, but the king's. A tear fell from his eye. From him! I couldn't believe this man cried. He looked at me with those wet obsidian eyes with such tenderness. Then he took my hand.

"I love you, Anna. My daughter. I hadn't seen you since

you were nine years old. You were so little. Now, you've grown. You should be proud of the woman you've become."

"I don't remember you visiting."

"Aye, it was the last games. It was to be in summer again last year, but, with the state of war looming, we changed the plan. But I came to see you."

"And Mother."

"Aye," he said with a nod. "Aye. And your mother. I love her so much too."

"I think you should see her on your last night here."

"Yeah?" he asked, lifting an eyebrow. "Hmm. Well, she and I had a bit of a falling out after you left. Your mother, you know, is a very strong-willed woman and doesn't like it when people differ from her opinions."

"I know."

We both laughed.

"Perhaps you're right, Anna." He got up. He was so tall that when we both rose, he was still a head taller than me. "All right. But not until after I get another hug from my daughter."

I gestured at something on his face. He leaned down a little, and I brushed the tear from his eye. Then I hugged him.

"Take care of yourself, Anne. I love you."

15

GOODBYE

IN THE MORNING, OUR BEACHES FELT SO SURREAL, WITH SO many of my Amazons still dressed formally in lovely peplos, their blue-tinted faces shining underneath our green sun, curled up in the arms of men in simple traveling tunics readying themselves to sail home. I couldn't spot the king . . . my father. He was probably already aboard one of the larger ships. But so many couples were frozen, before the purple waves, in the tightest embraces. It was depressing as Hades, I tell you. And even worse was the crying. There was so much sobbing, it made me feel awful. My friends were so right. Hanna, Iris, and Eva, and so many others, had refused to come, warning me to stay back in the palace. They knew what the last day of the games was all about. It wasn't farewell—it was a well of tears.

"Goodbye, Marcus," I said, sounding far more sad and formal than I had intended. Then I put out my hand to shake.

Marcus whirled around, dropping the bag from his shoulder on the purple sand. Then he sort of stared at my hand. The two older men accompanying him continued walking to the closest ship beached on the shore. I really had come down to find Felix. Instead I had found . . .

Marcus. He bent down on one knee, snatched my hand, and kissed the back of it.

"My greatest honor this Olympiad was seeing you, princess."

"Oh, stop," I snapped, snatching my hand back. "You're acting like a fool."

He stood up and shook his head. Then I extended my arms and we embraced.

"I'll miss you," I whispered in his ear.

"Even after our fight?" he asked. "I'm surprised you're still talking to me. What I did was vulgar but, oh Avva, I was so mad at your challenge. It was better than what I really wanted to do, had you been a man. Then your lovely face would have met my fists."

"You mean what I did to you after?"

"Aye . . ." And then he chuckled. "You clocked me good." And he put his hand out again to shake. "Friends?"

"Friends."

"Marcus, bring in more of the nymphs' ropes from the tents to ready our ship, won't you?" cried another boy. I'd know that voice anywhere. Of all men, it was Felix! He was carrying a whole handful of bags down a sandy dune toward the ships. "Your father wants us to be ready. By the gods, who knows what mischief Poseidon is planning when we cross. We might not live to see battle again."

I felt my face burn red. But Felix was none the wiser. Perhaps he had thought I was Hanna or another nymph? It was only when I turned around and he finally recognized me that he dropped his bags on the purple sand, just as Marcus had. And then he, too, stared at me in shock.

"Anna?"

I looked at Marcus. Now both my favorite men were standing beside me on the beach.

"I'm surprised the two of you talk to one another," I quipped.

"Aside from the games," Felix said, putting an arm around Marcus, "we fight on the same team. I told you that, Anna."

"Says you," Marcus said, pushing him off with a laugh. Felix almost fell on the sand and, for a flash, it looked like Felix wanted to charge him. But then Felix smiled at me.

"There be nothing more fanciful in your lands than you, Anna," Felix said, straightening his tunic and bowing before me.

I laughed.

"Stuff it, Felix," Marcus said. "The princess came over to say goodbye to *me*."

"No," I replied, "I came to say goodbye to both of you. When will I be seeing you again? I so wish you could stay in Azure."

"Hopefully sooner rather than later," Felix said.

"Depending on the tide of war," Marcus said, turning serious.

We lost our smiles.

"Everyone aboard," hollered a gray-haired man in gilded armor. He was standing on the bow of one of the ships beached on the purple sand. "Come on. Time to leave! By the gods, you've all said your goodbyes long enough. Shedding enough sarding tears to flood the Napean shore. Keep it up and I won't have to weigh anchor."

"Brasius," Marcus muttered beneath his breath and spit on the sand. "That old craggy tight-in-the-pants idiot loves the sea, even if it's only sailing across a few waves."

"He's a tyrant," said Felix with a nod, staring at him. "But he'll be sailing in our ship, thanks to your father."

"You two *are* friends, aren't you?" I asked, looking at them, astonished.

Marcus smirked but shook his head. "Never friends enough to share a princess."

"Aye," Felix said, "upon the next Olympiad, I so look forward to spending time alone with you again, Anna."

"I heard about that," Marcus said, scowling. "Perhaps we should fight for her now, Felix?"

"How about I decide when you both return," I replied. "Oh, I'm going to miss both of you so much." Then I kissed Felix's cheek. And then Marcus's. But then I felt a tear fall from my eye. "Goodbye, guys."

"Goodbye, Princess Avivae," said Marcus.

"Bye, Anna," said Felix with a nod.

"Bye, Felix."

And then . . . oh, saying goodbye to them was all just so depressing!

16

GOODBYE, ALREADY

So there I stood at the top of the great spiral steps, staring across the grand hall and through the three-story window at the Strait, with my chin leaning on my hands, feeling miserable. I ran a hand through my long black hair and sighed. I suppose, had it been the previous day, I would have seen the ships sailing back across the sea. Not today. Today it was a beautifully clear day with the sun's green rays shining on our blue fields and on the forest trees separating us from the distant purple sands of our shore.

Our empty shore.

No matter how many times you say goodbye, people still leave. The games, the festival, the men, all of it, had left. Now the palace was back to normal everyday drudgery, with all my sisters walking with a little less pep in their step than a fortnight before. They were down too. All of Azure, if you can imagine, had become more *blue*.

After leaning on the golden rail at the top of the inner gallery for forever, I caught my mother passing the guards below. She was dressed formally, as always, with her long hair wrapped in a black cloth and a long light-blue dress flowing along the marble floor as she slowly climbed the steps. Then she stood beside me at the top of the stairs.

She offered me something in her hands. It was a quill, ink, and scroll. Then she turned from me and stared out the window with me.

"Write."

"What?"

"Write, Avivae. I've seen you write many times in your room. Write. I do that too, for your father."

"What?" I thought she was crazy. I just squinted at her.

"Write to him. It will make the distance seem shorter. It is what I do all the time."

"What are you talking about?" I snapped, annoyed. She pushed the scroll to my chest again, smiled ruefully, and just nodded.

"Whenever I think of your father, which is often, I take ink to the parchment and write to him. It makes me feel better. And then—" Her smile became wider, which made me more suspicious. "I send my letter by Imada across the Strait, by air, to be delivered to your father's castle tower in Castle Cove. It's been like this since before you were born. I write to him nearly every moon, and he answers me just as often."

"Is this supposed to make me feel better?"

"Just write to Felix and all will be better. You will see."

I faced her. I felt the heat rush to my face again. "What makes you think I'd write to Felix? Perhaps I'd write to Father."

She looked surprised. My mother's veins ran so cold that I rarely saw much emotion. She infernally turned back toward the huge window looking over our glorious view of the sea and nodded, staring out with me. Then, after a long silence, she spoke again. I was beginning to wish she hadn't.

"Suit yourself," she said with a shrug. "Write to whoever you'd like."

"They say," Mother said, still looking at the view, "Harmonia designed this lookout in order to look upon the continent of Atala. It is said she was as interested in man as we are. Her daughter loved a man far south in Egypt. All members of the Ambrosia family have fallen in love with men from across the Strait. But Harmonia knew that an Amazon's life was better lived alone."

"How is it better, Mother?" I snapped. "Now that you ordered everyone to leave?"

She nodded and muttered, "I suppose we're even. I was furious when Daphne died."

"Don't you dare bring that up. Not now."

"Let me finish," she said, equally perturbed, raising a hand.

The cuff on her wrist fit perfectly and accentuated the formality of her dress. Her formal dress. Every day she dressed in perfect royal clothes, never showing the least informality. Always perfect. We couldn't be any more different. I wore the clothes of our people. A simple brown leather tunic and pants with my long curly hair flowing, in knots today, down to my shoulders.

"What happened before," she said, "that thing I won't say for your sake, and then your victory afterward, has settled a score. I told you at supper that you brought great honor to me and our people by winning that match. That made up for . . . that thing you don't want me to talk about."

I smiled at her efforts to not offend me.

"Thanks. But I'm sorry for you, Mother. I'm sorry Father had to go."

That seemed to upset her a lot. Her eyes opened wide for a moment. I watched her clench the rail tightly, and then she turned back to the window and quietly nodded.

"Avva, as difficult as you find me, my mother Dainya lived according to the law. She placated the gods, doing everything according to the laws of Olympus for centuries. And I never once disobeyed her—" She cocked her head and smirked. "I suppose, mild transgressions here and there, but I never really disobeyed her. She . . . wouldn't even talk to me like I am doing with you now. All my life, I strived to be as perfect as my mother. Indeed, Dainya lived many centuries due to her perfection. The only time I ever dared defy her laws was in regard to your father. But by then, she had passed away, betrayed by the gods. I suppose her death drove me to a fit of stupid rebellion. I shall pay my due. But—"

"You don't have to tell me all this."

"You need to understand so that you can understand me."

I would never understand her.

"Like I said," I replied, pushing her parchment back to her chest, "you're the one who needs to be consoled, not me, Mother. You go write. You kept these laws that have kept men far away from us."

She didn't grab the scroll and quill, and they just fell to the ground. Neither of us picked them up. Instead, Mother turned back to the view, leaned on the rail, and infernally just slowly nodded again.

"I didn't write that law, Avivae. Neither did Nefertiti. The gods did."

"Engel and Father told me that. You suffer as much as I do, if not worse, Mother."

"Okay," she said and patted my hand on the rail. "Glad to have talked to you." Then she started walking back down the stairs.

Wait! That's it? How typical. This conversation is probably the most I'll get from her for the next decade. So I yelled, "Where are you going!"

"I'm leaving," she said with a chuckle. But she stopped a few steps down. "Now that we finally spoke—"

"You call that speaking? You think everything's resolved?"

"Avva," she said, shaking her head, "I don't know what you want from me."

"When I am queen, Mother, I will not subjugate my

people and imprison them behind the Strait. Hades or not, the gods or not, my people will be set free. I will get rid of this edict. They will travel to Southern Atala and see their families, their husbands. And they will not be left alone to care for their children ever again."

"Then you will curse our people. And with it, you will destroy Azure Blue."

But then she actually laughed. I wasn't sure what to do with that. Even the guards at the base of the stairs glanced up.

"But you would, wouldn't you, Avivae? You would fight the gods themselves. You're the most stubborn child a mother could hope for. I hate to think it, but I believe you will do this."

"I will."

"Is it all so bad?" she asked, heaving a sigh. "You and I had Engel. Engel is more than most people could ask for in their childhood. And, anyway, your father, even without the edict, wouldn't have come home. Even if I abolished the law, as you say you'll do, he and the rest of man are far too busy fighting. So, I ask again, what can I give you?"

She waited for a response but then quietly nodded and started back down the stairs.

"*A mother!*"

"What?" She stopped cold midway down the steps.

"You asked me what I want? I want *a mother*." My voice breaks. "That's it. I want *a mother* from you."

"What does that even mean?" she asked with a furrowed brow. "You have a mother. And a father too now. You know, your father lives far away across the sea, but at least you know him. I think he comes here more to see you than me. I never even met my father."

"I see what you like in him. His energy. His heart. He's everything you aren't."

"He's not so great, Avivae," she said with a chuckle. "You only knew him for a fortnight, I've known him far longer. He's a king living in a violent world who has to hang the enemy every day. He has to be ruthless and brutal in order to survive."

"But he has energy. And he has heart."

"Aye," she said sadly with a nod. "Aye, that he does. He has heart." In silence, it looked like she was considering turning and leaving again. Then she cocked her head back in thought. "I suppose, if you'd like, you can't cross the sea, but perhaps Felix can. Perhaps I can arrange a visit for him in the future?"

I said nothing. Who in Hades cared about Felix?

"I was planning a celebration with our people for your win," she added formally. "I'm wondering if you'd like to join us so that I can congratulate you in front of the whole kingdom. You don't have to, but you'll be honored and I'd love to do it for you. There'd be myrle berry wine for the victor of the games. My daughter."

"Will Engel be there?"

"Of course."

I nodded.

She looked up at me. And then with distaste, she said, "But wear something nicer."

After she had descended the stairs, she vanished at a turn into another hall. I shouted out, "I'm sorry he had to leave you, Mother."

17

SEASHELLS

On another lovely day, long after the games, with our bright green sun beaming down, warming my long black hair and reflected off the sea, Hanna and I walked hand in hand on the purple sand. Sometimes we ran. The shimmering bright amethyst waves fell at our blue feet. She had come up with the idea of collecting seashells. She wanted to make a necklace for her mother's birthday. Our chores were finished, and Engel had let us go early from our studies. So, my friend had begged me to fly Naya from the stables to the beach. We sat together on the short flight and landed the unicorn on the sand. Now, Naya was grazing among some bushes up the hills while we occasionally picked up a shell or two.

It was hot. Soon it would be summer. I was thankful for wearing pants. Hanna wore a long blue dress, and her hands were getting clammy and a bit drippy.

"I heard," Hanna said, "that General Onos might visit soon, Blue. He's coming to talk with Cambria and the Imada about the war."

"So?"

"So, well, you know, where we find the general . . . we might find the general's son, *right?*"

"Oh, come on. Are you still stricken by Marcus?" I asked, grabbing my hand back. "I thought you weren't." I examined her eyes. "Hanna, forget him. You won't see him till he's old and gray with children and married to some old hag. We're not going to ever see them."

"*How can you say that!*" And she looked furious.

"I was just saying," I said with a shrug. I gazed at the beautiful waves coming and crashing to the sand. Then I felt the water spray over my cheeks. "Why don't we swim? I think it's getting—"

"How could you say that, Avva!"

"Are you serious? What do you think? They're going to war. We might not see Marcus or Felix or any of the boys for another three years, or . . . ever."

"Oh, Avva! Sometimes you can be so awful! Well, if you're right, you might not see your father either!"

That wasn't nice. That was really mean. I had told her about Darius. How could I not? Hanna was my best friend, and I confided in her everything. And she was the only nymph I had told my secret about my father.

I tried to shrug off her words and kept staring out to the sea. I didn't respond because I didn't want to fight.

"Sorry," she said, touching my arm. "I didn't mean that."

"It's all right. I deserved it, I suppose." I reached down and picked up some purple sand and let it run through my fingers. That made me think about what Engel had once said. He said that sand in the yellow lands is white. I couldn't imagine white or yellow sand. "I've written to him, you know."

"Felix?"

"Not Felix, stupid. My father."

"Did he write back?"

"A couple times. Cambria says he's so busy. I've heard that the enemy is amassing close to the border of Crescent Blue. That's why Onos is coming to a secret meeting with Cambria and the Imada. Word is, Delia might need to send the Imada by monokera to fly across the Strait. No Amazon has fought in a war for centuries. But if any fall, you know, Hanna, our immortal sisters shall finally die, just like in the games."

"Well, you don't have to be so depressing about it all. Men war all the time. It's what they do. And at least, Avva, you can write to the king."

"Yeah, but it's not enough."

"Here's one!" Hanna cried, becoming giddy. She picked something up from the sand and jumped up, clapping. She handed it to me. It was an amethyst shell, the size of my thumb, that sparkled under the green sunlight. The center was multicolored like a rainbow.

"Yes, that's a lovely one."

"Maybe we can put this in the center? Cambria told me she has an old pearl. But wouldn't it be nice, Avva, to put a pearl in the center? Maybe we can find a pearl. But if we don't, I think this will do nicely."

I smiled. I had always been impressed by how little it took to make Hanna happy. I wished simple stuff like that would settle me down. My mind was always jumpy.

"One day, Hanna, I'll see him in the yellow lands across the sea . . . One day. And one day, I'll visit his castle at Castle Cove in Azerban. He told me how beautiful it is."

She wasn't listening. She was wiping the purple sand off the shell with her blue fingers. Then she threw it with the others in the bag on her back.

"Iris wants to do your hair," Hanna added, seeming to search the ground even more carefully after her prized find. "And—" She looked at me with a big grin and I giggled. "She's really good at it now. I think you should let her."

"If she wants a challenge."

Then I muttered, more to myself than to her, staring out across the sea, through a blue haze, at the yellow-brown continent on the other side, "Perhaps I'll take Naya or Ranun or even Antilus there. Sure, the Strait isn't that far by air. We see their yellow and brown shores all the time. The water might be rough, but I could get there from the sky above. Then I could travel to the kingdom and travel back. Why, Mother might not even need to know I left."

I thought Hanna wasn't listening. Certainly, she must be too focused on hunting for shells for her mother's necklace. But when I turned from the waves back to my friend, I saw that was wrong. She was staring at me like I had completely flipped my lid.

"You can't ever do that," she said with wide eyes. "Are you crazy?"

"You know I am." I put my hand on her shoulder, and we giggled. I pointed toward the forest. "Let's go up closer, up toward the hill over there. I remember a pile of shells on the sand. I know we can find an alabaster one. Or perhaps even one that's blue."

THE END

AVVA'S ADVENTURES ARE CONTINUED IN THE NEXT BOOK IN THE SERIES, AZURE BLUE

THE AZURE SERIES

- HARMONIA
- CORA: RISE OF THE FALLEN GODDESS
- AZURE BLUE
- CORAL RED

And don't forget to check out the audiobook version of Princess Sojourn, narrated by Alexa Elmy, soon to be available on all retailers!

PARTING WORDS

What did you think of *Princess Sojourn*? By placing a book review, you can inform others of your thoughts and help spread the word about my book.

Want more? Periodically I like to send news regarding current or new projects. If you'd like to be privy, I encourage you to sign up to my email newsletter. Your information will remain private and you can cancel any time.

Sign up at www.alhawke.com or scan the following QR code:

EXCERPT FROM AZURE BLUE

"CHAPTER 1 - AVVA" IN AZURE BLUE, BOOK 2 OF THE AZURE BLUE SERIES BY A.L. HAWKE

Avva awoke early in the morning with her heart pounding. She was so excited. Today was the day. She would fly Antilus across the Strait to the Hinterlands, the lands of her father. She would go with her best friend, Hanna (though it would take a bit more coaxing).

She had always thought Hades' edict was a myth. How could the god of the Underworld magically take away a nymph's immortality just for traveling across the Strait? She would prove it was a lie. And if she was wrong and the edict was true, she would live decades rather than centuries. So what? Then she'd be human like her father.

She stood in front of a tall vanity mirror. She dressed in travel clothes—a simple brown leather tunic, pants, and boots. She straightened her long curly black hair over her pointy nymph ears. As she carefully applied makeup, she heard footsteps from behind. Engel hobbled in.

"Don't you knock?" Avva asked, not turning fully around.

Engel was a short old dwarf. Mother called him a Mandrigel, whatever that was. He had blue skin like Avva's, but whereas on her it was barely noticeable, his entire face was bright blue. His hair was thin and gray. He stood a little under four feet tall and had stubby fat fingers, long bushy gray eyebrows, and a fat, broad nose. He didn't walk, he hobbled. He was wise, kind, and cute. She adored him.

"Princess, it's early," Engel said kindly. "Where do you think you're going? There's more ceremony today."

She loved him more than anyone in the palace. He had raised her. It was said he had lived hundreds of years. His wisdom was completely contrary to his cuteness. And next to Avva, who now towered at nearly six feet, he looked like an ancient wrinkled child.

"I don't care," she said with a laugh, staring at a mirror. "After yesterday, I've had enough of ceremony. I'm going away somewhere, I suppose."

"Where?" he repeated, more sternly.

"Away." Avva turned and faced Engel. "Out. Get out of my room and leave me alone."

"Where, Blue?" he insisted, with his gentle tone again. "Tell me."

Avva placed a finger over her chin and pointed out the window. The window faced the purple grasslands, then beyond the forest, further to the sea. Of course, the act of pointing in that direction gave Engel not the slightest bit of information.

Engel snorted in anger. "Where, Avva? Your mother has asked for you to accompany her this afternoon. She wants to apologize. You think running off again is going to mend what's going on between you two?"

Avva sat in a gilded chair, shrugged, and turned away from him. She applied makeup to her cheeks. Then she thought of the burn on her face, the humiliation. So she angrily dipped her sponge in white makeup, absorbing way too much. She shrugged again and used it to cover all traces of blueness on her face.

"Don't worry," she said, patting her face. "It was nothing. I'm not a little girl."

Engel walked up closer. He stood beside her, level with her head as she sat. He put a hand on her shoulder. "Are you all right, Blue?"

His voice was so kind it made her feel that lump in her throat again.

"Why wouldn't I be?" She applied even more powder. She hated being a nymph. She wanted to be human. Like her father.

"I could help you, if you let me know where you're going."

Avva lifted her eyebrows. She smiled and turned to her friend.

"Yes. Yes, you can, Engel. Yes. Indeed. Would you be a dear and tell Her Majesty that my friend Hanna and I have decided to go hunting for lapis deer. Tell her it's the only way to get my mind off the terrible news about Father and … that other nasty thing that happened to me in Court yesterday."

"Okay. If you tell me where."

"Tell her the northern hills," she said with a shrug. "Or…" She put her finger to her chin again. "No, tell her we're going fishing under Mount Ambitus along the Stratos. That's it. We're going fishing along the Stratos."

"But where are you going *really*, Avva? Tell me the truth and I might do it."

Avva giggled and looked into his bright blue eyes. "The truth?"

He nodded.

"We're traveling across the Strait to visit my father's kingdom."

"You're not!" he yelled, and he snorted and stomped his feet. His face flashed red. She didn't think she had ever seen him so mad.

"I won't touch down."

"Avva." Engel said. He paused, seemingly gathering his thoughts. "The queen isn't herself. You must not do anything to upset her more. If you do this, I'll have the guards turn you back."

"The queen mourns in her way, I mourn my way. I wish to visit my father's kingdom, even if it's just to finally see it from the clouds. But tell her … tell her I'm going fishing along the Stratos. Not hunting, fishing. That's it. Tell her that, would you, Engel?"

"I won't!" Engel snorted. "It's forbidden. It is a law beyond your mother. I won't be a part of this silly talk."

He was about to say more when Avva raised her right hand. She became very serious. She stood up and walked over to her window with her back to him.

Engel didn't say another word. He wasn't prone to lecturing her. He probably figured she got enough of that from her mother.

"Engel," she said, wanting to change the subject. She tapped on her glass window. "Have you ever noticed how small the window in my room is?"

But when Avva turned, Engel was gone. She shrugged and walked to her nightstand to grab more things. Then the door creaked open and in came Hanna wearing similar leather travel clothes with her hair in a ponytail.

"You requested my presence, my lady?" Hanna gave a bow. They laughed.

"We must hurry," Avva said in a hushed voice. She ran back to her mirror and busied herself, working faster, covering up the final marks of blue along her ears.

"Are we really going through with this?"

"Yep. And I think our favorite dwarf plans on snitching. Are the monokera ready?"

"Yes. By the tower stables and ready to go." Hanna furrowed her brow and stared at Avva in the mirror. "What did you do to your face?"

"Taking off all this blue stuff." She looked up in thought. "I wonder what it's like, Hanna? I wonder what's over there?"

"They say the air changes. The sky, the grass, even the sun changes its hue to yellow. The sky is blue like our trees. And the air becomes thicker because it's not high up like Napea."

"Strange."

"Yeah." Hanna nodded and walked to the window. "They say the men are a strange race, always fighting. Strong people, some twice to three times the size of us."

"But cute, right?"

"Don't be stupid, Avivae," Hanna said with a laugh.

"Well, certainly there was something that attracted my mother."

"They're strong. Big. You saw the boys at the games. Their strongest could probably break you in half." Hanna looked up with dreamy eyes. "Some are gallant, some noble. Others are dumb and reckless. Fire, swords, land, that's the language of man."

"How exciting the day will be. Did you tell your mother?"

Hanna lost her wondrous gaze and turned grave. "Seriously, Avva, you need to promise me that you'll protect me from her. I could get into a lot more trouble than you."

"It's going to be so much fun." Avva nodded. Then she smiled slyly. "I'll tell you a little secret, Hanna." She put a finger to her lips and whispered, "I'm going to land."

"Sure, Blue," Hanna said, rolling her eyes.

"Let's go before Engel locks the tower stables."

They quickly climbed the spiral stone staircase up the south tower until reaching the summit of the crystal tower. Then they made their way across ramparts and a high bridge to enter the stables. A guard in ancient scarlet hoplite armor stood by the entrance, but she let them pass seeing it was the princess.

Avva flew Antilus harder this time. She wanted to make it to the beach more quickly than yesterday. It would be a long trip, and she wanted as much time as possible. Hanna, atop

Maythra, struggled to keep up. Antilus was the fastest of all the monokera.

It was still early morning when they reached the shore. The bright green sun was reflected by the purple sand.

They spotted two girls playing by the waves. They were sisters, Iris and Eva, a little younger than Avva. She had joined them in the castle for breakfast, with a few other nymphs, a week ago. The girls glimpsed their shadows as they flew over. Eva turned and looked up, curious, but their surprise turned to shock as Avva and Hannah left the beach and flew over the sea.

"We have to turn back," Hanna hollered through the wind, flying beside Avva. "We've been spotted."

"No."

"Avva, the girls will tell!" Hanna shouted. "We must." She turned her unicorn's head back to the shore. But Antilus was a royal unicorn, faster and stronger than any other unicorn in the kingdom. With ease, Avva flew ahead of Hanna and hovered in front of her, blocking her.

"What are you doing?" cried Hanna. "Get out of my way so I can fly back home! Please, Avivae."

"No!" Avva yelled back.

They hovered for a moment silently, hearing only the flapping of their unicorns' wings. Avva looked back. Indeed, Iris and Eva were shouting something at them in the distance.

"Avva, what's this about? This isn't funny anymore. We've been spotted. They'll go straight back to your mother and tell."

"I can't return. This is my only chance."

"Why? Tell me why, princess?"

"Just go back to the palace." Avva nodded solemnly. "I'll go the rest of the way myself."

"But why? Why are you doing this?"

"Just go back, Hanna."

"Tell me."

"I order you, as your princess, to return to the palace!" Avva demanded.

The words were so stern that Maythra started to obey. Hanna had to pull the unicorn's head back.

Hanna looked at Avva and bowed atop the unicorn in mockery. Then she frowned. "All right, *Your Highness*. I'll return. But, as your friend, I'd like to know why you won't come back with me."

"It was dumb to ask you to come along. I can't guarantee your safety. But Hanna, I've heard rumors in the Court. The queen intends to keep me grounded after yesterday. If I don't go, I may never be able to see my father's lands. I…"

She couldn't continue. She started crying. The tears came down hard. Now it seemed like she couldn't stop.

Hanna flew as close to her as she could. It looked like her friend wanted to comfort her.

"Oh, Avva, I'm so worried about you. I didn't want to go, but I came with you because of the scene in Court yesterday. But now you're scaring me. Are you really running away?"

"No. I'll be back. Don't worry."

"I'm so worried. Please, just come back with me now."

Avva shook her head.

"Then come back home soon."

Avva nodded. She slowly pulled her unicorn's neck away from her friend and headed toward the sea. At that moment, Avva's mind was made up. She wouldn't just fly over the foreign land, she'd land.

TO BE CONTINUED IN THE NEXT BOOK IN THE SERIES, AZURE BLUE

ALSO BY A.L. HAWKE

FANTASY: THE AZURE SERIES

- HARMONIA
- CORA: RISE OF THE FALLEN GODDESS
- AZURE BLUE
- CORAL RED

PARANORMAL ROMANCE

- THE HAWTHORNE UNIVERSITY WITCH SERIES (I-III)
- THE HAWTHORNE UNIVERSITY WITCH SERIES (4-6)
- SHADES
- HAUNTING JOY
- PHANTOM MASQUERADE

- MY EVIL EYE
- THE GUARDIAN
- NECTAR OF AMBROSIA
- CORA

SCIENCE FICTION

- CANDY SAVANT SERIES

Books available at https://alhawke.com/books

ABOUT THE AUTHOR

A.L. Hawke is the author of the bestselling Hawthorne University Witch series. The author lives in Southern California torching the midnight candle over lovers against a backdrop of machines, nymphs, magic, spice and mayhem. A.L. Hawke writes fantasy and romance spanning four thousand years, from pre-civilization to contemporary and beyond.

Visit A.L. Hawke at www.alhawke.com

Email: contact@alhawke.com

9 781953 919861